The Tapestry of Odette

Nika Engel

iUniverse, Inc.
New York   Bloomington

The Tapestry of Odette

iUniverse books may be ordered through booksellers or by contacting:

iUniverse
1663 Liberty Drive
Bloomington, IN 47403
www.iuniverse.com
1-800-Authors (1-800-288-4677)

Because of the dynamic nature of the Internet, any Web addresses or links
contained in this book may have changed since publication and may no longer be
valid. The views expressed in this work are solely those of the author and do not
necessarily reflect the views of the publisher, and the publisher hereby disclaims
any responsibility for them.

ISBN: 978-1-4502-4667-5 (sc)
ISBN: 978-1-4502-4671-2 (ebk)

Printed in the United States of America

iUniverse rev. date: 7/20/2010

CHAPTER 1

wo ist mein pferch?

I wonder what it is about being hurt that makes you want to hurt yourself even more. Odette wondered the same thing as she stared at her wan reflection in the bathroom mirror. A large kitchen knife hung loosely in her right hand, the blade still smeared with her blood. Red teardrops dripped slowly from the gashes on her left arm, spattering their scarlet stains across the pure white bathroom sink. Odette continued to stare at the mirror, even as it shimmered before her eyes, an unstable kaleidoscope of blood and water and flesh.

She laid the knife down on the edge of the sink, wincing at the soft metallic clatter. A flick of her trembling hand sent a rush of water down from the tap, swirling crimson lines down the gaping drain. Her arm felt numb, deadened nerves only registering a slight stinging on her skin. She ran her hands under the water; it was cold and clean, refreshing. Distracting even, but she could hardly remember what she was being distracted from.

A stray sound from outside her sealed sanctuary caused Odette to turn her head suspiciously, surveying the shut bathroom door. Leering horned faces grew and faded in the woodwork, lolling their fiery tongues at her. She ignored them, intently listening for any other noises that might signal an intruder. She quickly thrust the knife blade under the water tap, turning it this way and that to purge it of damning evidence. As soon as it was clean she pulled open a low drawer and slid it beneath a stack of clean peppermint-coloured towels, patting them down to show no disturbance. She slipped her thin arm beneath the water but withdrew it swiftly with a hiss as the stream stung at her myriad of cuts. She grabbed up a black sweater she had laid down on the ground earlier and slid it on, pulling the sleeves down to hide her self-mutilation.

She cracked the bathroom door slightly, poking her head out suspiciously. The narrow carpeted hallway was still dark, no signs of her foster parents or anyone else. She quickly turned off the running spigot and shut off the bathroom light, slipping across the hall into her room. The darkness swirled around her, threatening and overwhelming, but she didn't turn on the light in her room. She picked her way through the shadows to her bed and threw herself down on it. She could barely make out the clock she had hanging from the ceiling above her bed. Three hundred. With a sigh she buried her face in her pillow, ignoring the stinging that was starting to fester up in her arm. She closed her eyes, trying to fade away from everything around her. She could hear a steady thumping in the hall outside her door, like a man rhythmically driving a pole into the floor over and over and over. She knew from experience that covering her ears did nothing to dispel this sound, it would still echo from the insides of her palms, tormenting her into insanity. There were no traces of sleep or weariness in her mind, such things fled from her as eagerly as chaos pursued her. She tossed restlessly in bed, her frustration rising steadily as the hands of the clock chimed relentlessly onwards. The pole thumping continued to increase in volume until it was booming thunderously in her ears. She screwed her eyes tighter and tighter shut, but that just gave her a headache.

She wasn't sure of the exact moment that she slipped into slumber, but suddenly she found herself standing before a wall of tumbling colour. Reds, metallic hues, deep purples, soft greys, all rushing together in a cacophonous waterfall of brilliance. She stood entranced, just staring at it, as every shade known to man and bees rushed before her eyes, constantly changing and shifting. It put any rainbow she had seen to shame. Nothing was faded here, it was all bold and brilliant, dripping from the canvas of the gods before her enchanted eyes. It all mixed and swirled together, churning and pounding like the rapids of a river. Orange, forest green, bright pink, dun, differing shades of black, colours she couldn't even imagine, all tumbling together. It was awhile before she even noticed the ground beneath her feet, which was some sort of soft sucking mud. The two walls that angled away from the colour wall were both pitch black, made of shiny obsidian. They met together somewhere in the darkness, making the room a triangle. The ceiling was lost in the darkness, too vaulted to see.

Odette glanced only briefly at these other things, the colour wall kept inexorably drawing her gaze back to it. It was the most fascinating thing she had ever seen, it filled her heart and her mind and her soul all at once, satisfying her like opium. She began to slowly step towards it, wondering if she could touch it. She was only a few strides away, and she outstretched her finger, hypnotically drawn closer and closer to it.

"Odette," a distant voice called her name. It was harsh and rasping, shockingly unfamiliar. She didn't even pay attention to it at first, but it continued to cry her name, sounding more urgent with each shout. She paused her movement towards the wall, looking around her for the source of the voice. The light cast by the rushing colours only extended a few metres past her, everything beyond that was lost in darkness.

"Odette," the voice wailed again, sounding closer this time. She was almost fully turned away from the entrancing wall now, peering into the darkness, unable to make out anything.

"Hello?" she whispered. She felt as if she were in a library, or a cathedral. The voice seemed to have fallen silent, so she turned back to the wall, enthralled by its splendour. The soft brown mud sucked beneath her feet, grasping at her shoes. The silence around her was overwhelming, oppressing her mind with its presence. Suddenly a claw like hand shot out from the blackness and gripped her shoulder, as the hoarse voice croaked her name again. She whirled around, screaming, but the room shimmered and faded away.

The clock on her ceiling read six hundred. A soupy grey fog hung outside her window, blotting out all daylight. With a weary sigh, Odette swung out of her bed, grimacing. Her left arm ached, the pain finally registering in her abused nerves. She ignored it as she always did, aided by the fresh memories of the colour wall racing through her mind. She pulled on a pair of jeans and a new t-shirt and stumbled downstairs sleepily, yawning all the way. Her foster father, Dieter Schiller, sat in his recliner chair, watching football on the small box television. He was a friendly-looking man, with short blonde hair and stubble on his face. He had a slight paunch that was barely noticeable under the collared shirts he wore. Odette murmured good morning to him as she passed him; she tried to avoid speaking with both her foster parents as much as possible.

Her foster mother, Marie, was bustling about in the kitchen, washing the dishes from yesterday's supper. "Good morning, Odette," she said, flashing a smile. She smiled too much for Odette's liking, and the girl murmured an ingenuous reply. Maybe someday something bad would happen to her and then she might quit smiling all the time. The Schillers weren't bad foster parents, they left her alone most of the time, which she liked. She was fifteen years old and had been in twenty-one foster homes in the last four years. There was always something they couldn't deal with, the sullen silences, the self-mutilation, the hallucinations. Nobody wanted to deal with a schizophrenic orphan. Odette choked down her standard breakfast of oatmeal and bread and her morning supply of pills, before grabbing a brown jacket and silently exiting out the back door. She always walked to school, they only lived three blocks away from it. The air was cold outside, but not intolerable. Odette liked the cold, it was sharp and refreshing. Her white shoes slapped softly against the winter-hardened concrete, a soothing sound.

She was a small girl, with short dyed black hair curled around her face. She was a great deal prettier than she considered herself to be, in a dark Gothic way. She wore blue nail polish, black lipstick, and black eyeliner, circling her wide blue eyes. She wore two small butterflies in her ears and a bejewelled black choker. Her clothes were mostly pink or black, her two favourite colours. Her skin was pale and clear, sharply offset by all the darkness she surrounded herself with. She fervently hated her body; she thought her breasts were too small and her nose too stubbed, among a dozen other faults she found with her physical form.

"Odette," a soft voice called from behind her. She stopped but didn't turn around, listening to the quick steps approaching. Within moments a devilishly smiling heart-shaped face appeared at her shoulder, crowned by spiky black hair.

"Hey, Anna," Odette said, in a voice barely above a whisper. Anna didn't say anything, just fell into step besides Odette, studying her with bright blue eyes. She was a year older than her friend, but a head shorter. Despite her diminutive stature, an aura of quiet power surrounded her, an influential charisma. She the wore same black lipstick and eyeliner as Odette; she had inspired much of the rebellion in the younger girl. Around her neck she sported an aggressive spiked collar, made of bright stainless steel. Her eyes always seemed cloaked, as if she was shrouding some smouldering secret behind them. She still lived with her birth parents, who were horribly disappointed in her, which pleased her to no end. Her father was a wealthy banker and her mother was a computer saleswoman, so she had never really known want. Both her parents were religious types, and prayed to God to save their errant daughter's soul every night. Neither of them understood what fuelled her anger at the world, but she didn't want them to. It was something she barely understood it herself, but she knew it was an indelible part of her essence. Anna wasn't the sort of person to shy away from something she might find frightening; she had embraced her anger whole-heartedly. Odette adored her, both of them had been loners most of their lives, rejected by and rejecting society. Now they had formed what most of the adults in their lives considered an unhealthy friendship. But her parent's displeasure with it only served to cement Anna's fondness for Odette.

"I had a weird dream last night," Odette said slowly.

"Yeah?" Anna said, turning her inscrutable eyes back on her friend. She knew there had been something wrong.

"Well, I'm not sure if it was a dream or not," Odette continued, speaking quietly as if embarrassed. "It was more like a feeling, I guess. I saw all these colours and I knew they all meant something, they all made me feel something, but I couldn't figure out which was which before it was over."

"What colours?" Anna asked.

"Every colour," Odette chewed over every word. "Some I can't even remember . . . I think it was a dream."

"Dreams can be really fucked up," Anna said airily. "I have a dream where I have this black dog and I keep killing people with a golf club. It was fucking great."

"That's weird," Odette agree. "Though maybe not so much for you." She smiled as Anna rolled her eyes.

Odette hated school and rarely paid attention to anything that was taught there. She almost never did better than an eleven on any test, and most of her teachers thought it would take close to a miracle for her to graduate from Gymnasium. She didn't care though, school was simply torture, and something it was best to ignore and escape from. Anna shared these beliefs, although she usually garnered significantly better grades than Odette. It was the best way to keep her parents quiet and out of interfering with her life. Odette, on the other hand, found that foster parents rarely cared how she scored on such and such or whatever test, as long as she wasn't expelled from school.

She sat and watched an orange butterfly the size of her head float around the room, its dozen bulbous eyes rolling back and forth. Mrs. Müller was scribbling on the chalkboard at the front of the class, prattling on about Friedrich Barbarossa and his relationship with Henry the Lion or something like that. The butterfly landed on the pile of books on Odette's desk, antennas wavering in the air.

"Karl's soul is trying to run away, but they put a chain on it," it said, lifting up and hovering right in front of Odette's eyes, wings fluttering madly up and down until they were just a blur. Odette knew well enough by now not to respond to a hallucination in class, so she just nodded at it. The butterfly stared at her, its black eyes turning white. "What do you think Alexander is going to do with Karl now?"

Odette shrugged, looking off at the class room windows. This vision was starting to disconcert her. When she looked back it was gone, in a trail of white smoke.

Odette sat in her therapist's office, uncomfortably perched on a pale blue sofa. Her therapist, Stefani, was a tall blonde woman in her late twenties who smiled far too much for Odette's liking, just like Marie. She guessed that it was meant to be reassuring, but smiles never had that effect on Odette. She could see a brown folder with her name printed on it lying on Stefani's desk. Odette Braun.

"How have you been doing, Odette?" Stefani asked, her voice dripping honey. Odette shrugged, her eyes wandering off to Stefani's heavy-laden book shelves. Half of them were in English, which Odette couldn't read, so she perused Stefani's German collection. Die Traumdeutung, Zur Psychopathologie des Alltagslebems, Totem und Tabu, Das Ich und das Es, Die Zukunft einter Illusion. None of these were remotely interesting to Odette, and her eyes wandered away.

"Odette?" Stefani repeated.

"I've been OK," Odette replied, suddenly aware of the silence. "I had trouble sleeping last night."

"Why?"

"The thumping . . . and I had some weird dreams." Odette shifted on the sofa, suddenly feeling a sense of unease.

"What happened in the dreams?" Stefani had her pen and notepad out. Odette always hated that she was writing down everything she said. It made her feel like she was being interrogated.

"I can't remember exactly," Odette lied. "I was in a room and there was mud on the floor, I can remember that." She didn't feel like telling Stefani about the colour wall. It felt too important to disclose to anyone except Anna.

"And the thumping? Was it the same as usual?" Stefani was always interested in the noises that plagued Odette's attempts at sleep.

"Yeah," Odette's eyes wandered around the office again. It was small, with green paint and strange psychedelic paintings on the walls. The bookshelves and Stefani's desk were both chestnut brown; the desk held a computer monitor, a pile of folders, and a framed photograph of Stefani and her husband. Odette wondered what it would be like to be married to a therapist. Probably hell. They looked happy enough in the picture though. Stefani looked up from scratching on her notepad. "What do you suppose that means?" she asked.

Odette shrugged. "I'm not sure . . . its just annoying."

"Does it remind you of anything? Something from when you were little perhaps?"

Odette shook her head. "No, it doesn't mean anything to me. Its just . . ." Stefani had asked her these questions before. Did she really expect a different answer?

"Just what?" Stefani asked after a moment.

"I don't know," Odette snapped, tears springing to the back of her eyes. "I don't understand it. I don't understand anything."

"That's OK, Odette," Stefani smiled. "Have you been taking your medication?"

Odette nodded. Thank God for perphenazine. It kept her out of a mental institute, and in school, which she wasn't entirely sure was an improvement. She was pretty sure she would end up in an asylum before too long, regardless.

"Is there anything you would like to talk about?" Stefani asked. She asked this question every session too, and the answer, once again, was always the same.

"Not really," Odette replied, closing her eyes. She hated therapy, she had been drowned in it since she was a little girl.

"How have your hallucinations been?" Stefani was unfazed by Odette's unwillingness to participate.

"I've had some today. A butterfly talked to me," Odette smiled vaguely. She always felt as if she was teetering on the brink of incarceration, more here than any other place. She felt like a mouse being toyed with by a cruel cat. A cruel cat with a reassuring smile.

"What did it say?"

"Something about somebody named Karl," Odette said slowly. "It didn't make any sense."

"Do you remember what it said about Karl? I would like to know, even if it doesn't make a lot of sense," Stefani was scribbling on her notepad again.

Odette gritted her teeth. "It said something about him being chained up and then it asked me what we should do with it. Like, I guess it said Alexander chained Karl."

"Do you know who Alexander or Karl are?" Scratch, scratch, scratch.

"No," said Odette, trying to refrain from covering her ears.

"I can't recall you talking about butterflies before. Do you find that interesting?"

"Not really," Odette answered honestly. Couldn't they just lock her up in a little grey room and be done with it already?

"What do you suppose a butterfly means? Is it a symbol of happiness for you?"

These questions were annoying, but Odette hid her frustration. "I like them, I suppose. They're pretty."

"So it was a friendly vision?"

"Yeah, I guess you could say that. It didn't scare me, at least."

"Don't you think that's a good thing?"

Odette paused for a moment, thinking over the strange messenger. "It didn't make me feel good."

"And how did it make you feel?" Scratch, scratch, scratch.

"Nervous, I suppose."

"Do you know what it was about that butterfly that made you nervous?"

"Well, it was huge, and orange, and it had all these eyes, like a spider. And they kept all staring in different directions, and changing colour. I didn't like the way it looked at me, it was creepy. I think the whole thing was creepy, but it didn't scare me. It just made me . . . nervous." Odette desperately hoped that this explanation would please Stefani. The therapist said nothing for a moment, scribbling in her obligatory little notepad.

"Do you find that interesting?" she finally said, with an annoying smile.

"No," Odette replied flatly. "I don't."

Stefani's smile faltered slightly, then reformed resolutely. "Is there anything else you would like to talk about before we finish up?" Odette shook her head wordlessly. "Alright," Stefani continued. "I'll see you next Monday then, OK?"

CHAPTER 2

geisteskrankheit ist zufluchtsort

"I hate Stefani," Odette complained, perched on Anna's bed. "She's always smiling and asking me if I find something interesting and asking me the same stupid questions over and over."

Anna lay on the floor, staring at the roof, inhaling a cigarette. "I hate it when people smile all the time," she said. "Its so fake. Nobody's that fucking happy." Anna had wanted to paint her room black, but her parents had forbid it, so she plastered the sky blue walls with posters of obscure Gothic metal bands instead. A black cloth was draped over her dresser, holding several burning candles. Another candle sat on her bed stand, along with a knife, an ashtray, and a Koran. Anna wasn't a Muslim, but the presence of that book disconcerted her parents, which brought her a great deal of joy. Her bed had a dark red comforter, the colour of thick oozing blood, and carved black wooden bedposts. The carpet was beige, stained with cigarette ash and cut up in several places. Anna rolled on her side to look at Odette, gleefully putting out her cigarette on the carpet. "Toss me that knife," she said, indicating the dagger lying on the bed stand. She had bought it in some Turkish shop; the blade was curved and shiny, with a white ivory handle and a carved elephant head for a pommel. Anna smiled wryly as Odette took it gingerly by the handle and leaned forward to proffer it to her friend.

"Don't be so timid, darling," she said, grasping it with authority and cutting the air with it a few times, before laying the blade sideways across her arm. The candlelight played off it in the darkness, reflecting a silver sheen across the room. "You should cut me."

"What?" Odette said, starting slightly.

"You should cut me," Anna repeated dryly, another strange smile playing on her lips. "It would feel liberating."

Odette stared at the shining knife blade in horror. Anna turned it back and forth, running the sharp edge across her skin. Odette winced at the papery sound it made. Anna reversed the dagger, proffering the handle back to her friend. "No," Odette said, shaking her head for emphasis. "I can't do that, Anna, I . . ."

"Come on," Anna's voice sounded pleading, but she still had a wicked smile dancing across her face. Odette folded her arms around her body and shook her head wordlessly, looking down at her lap. She heard Anna's audible sigh of disappointment and the soft thunk with which the knife fell to the carpet. She looked up timidly to see Anna produce a dark blue lighter from her jeans pocket. She casually flicked it on a couple times, her look of dissatisfaction rapidly overcome by another evil little grin, her stare transfixed by the flickering little flame. Like a girl hypnotised she placed her palm over the dancing orange siren, moaning softly as it burned her flesh. The ashen smell filled up Odette's nostrils, as a loud clicking sound consumed her hearing. She clamped her hands over her ears automatically, in a vain effort to shut out a noise that emanated from inside her mind.

"That's like fucking sex," Anna sighed, staring at the bright red mark on her palm. She flicked the lighter teasingly at Odette, who slowly released her ears. "Come on, don't you want a preview, babe?"

She tossed the lighter to her friend, who caught it, fumbling it clumsily in her pale hands, but recovering it before it dropped into her lap. "Show a little spirit, darling," Anna whispered erotically, drawing a little closer to the bed, a strange light burning in her eyes as she watched Odette flick the lighter on and stare at the flame dance about, dying and being reborn. A long moment passed before Odette resolutely stuck her arm out, turning it upside down, and pushed the lighter against her flesh. It was intensely hot, and it hurt, intensely, but it was that good sort of pain; it made her flinch and smile at the same time. The smell of scorched flesh hit her with renewed force, but it didn't bother her this time, she almost drank it in. It was a wonderful aroma, a charred stink of death and pain that had to be savoured, like fine wine. She realised she had shut her eyes and was sighing, the lighter lying loosely in her palm. She flickered her eyelids open to catch the flash of the knife blade in Anna's left hand, and a devilishly happy look in her eyes. Anna stretched her right hand out to touch Odette's knee. "Give me your wrist, love," she whispered. "That was awesome, wasn't it?"

Odette nodded mutely, but made no move to obey Anna's request. She felt a tear spring to the back of her eye. Anna was so beguiling, humming soothingly, entrancingly, but Odette could still see the menace of the deadly sharp dagger clutched in her long pale fingers. The smell of burning skin began to overwhelm her, filling her head with smoke and ash and screaming death. Skulls flashed behind the back of her eyes, filling her vision with their stark white grins. Slowly she began to stretch her hand out, as if something compelled her imperiously. Centimetre by centimetre it drifted forward, with agonisingly slow speed. Anna licked her lips with a crimson tongue, turning her hand upwards to receive Odette's offering. After what seemed an eternity of floating in a cradle of smoke, Odette felt Anna's cold touch as their skin pressed together, and then fingers wrapping in an iron grip around her wrist. Her eyes, which had faded shut again, snapped open with alacrity that sent her mind into spinning shock, even as she saw the shimmering blade raised in the murky air.

Candlelight flickered and reflected across the walls, illuminating Anna's indescribable expression and her hungry weapon for the single second before she brought it down across Odette's arm with a delicate rush. The pain barely registered on Odette's drowsing nerves, but the scarlet splash of blood flashed across her vision, framed against the backdrop of darkness. She felt her stomach lurch and the room swam before her, mixing the scarlet into the beige, the black, and the orange pin pricks of candlelight. Anna leaned down to softly lap up the blood that trickled from Odette's arm, running her tongue sensually across her friend's pale skin. In that moment, the blackness of the multitudinous posters grew with jarring rapidity, swallowing up all the other colours, and leaving only an abyss of sight and feeling.

Odette stood before the colour wall, gasping in the thick air. At first it strongly resembled Anna's room; orange, black, silver, and white, with the odd dash of royal purple, but then it changed. Greens came rushing in, and earthy browns, mixed in with sky and navy blues, gold, and russet. Odette shifted in the mud, feeling it squelch beneath her socked feet. She didn't look down at it, once again she felt helpless to tear her gaze from the mesmerising wall. It encompassed everything she could comprehend, the feelings that coursed through her body were almost too numerous for her to register, they came and went with the passing of each splash of colour. Joy, anger, pain, fear, jealousy, love, hatred, delight, content, lust; she felt as if her heart would burst as conflicting emotions tore at it, threatening to consume it in one massive rush of blood and thought. She tried to shut her eyes to stem the flood, if even for a moment, so that she could breathe again, but the hypnosis of the wall did not even allow her that respite. She felt as if her eyelids were nailed to her brow, and they remained as unmoving as lead. Pink, metallic blue, dark forest green, an unknown colour that she couldn't put a name to. Each brought a new avalanche of emotion that crashed through her body, leaving her rent and trembling. She tried to beat them back, to control them somehow, but they continued to run rampant, reckless, through her soul and heart. Fires started to burn in the corridors of her mind, wild and out of control. She heard screaming and smelled the stench of burning flesh, pervading all of her senses. She could feel the flickering on her fingertips, hanging limply at her side, but she couldn't even gather the strength to look down.

The wall consumed everything, whispering dark secrets in languages that she couldn't understand. Etsiä avain. She collapsed to her knees, but her gaze did not for one second flicker from the colours that held her in absolute thrall. The hues shifted again; ashen grey, milky white, copper, a sickening shade of yellow-green. The tips of her fingers went numb, as unrecognisable feelings ravaged her soul, ripping through the interiors of her consciousness. *A minha senhora de morte.* Whispers echoed through the darkness of her mind, somewhere in the caverns where her inner vision couldn't pierce. She couldn't even blink now, her eyelids felt sluggish, embedded in hardened concrete. She felt a single tear trickle down her cheek, and her lips moved to whisper a single word to the animate colours. "Please," it sounded so soft that she could barely hear herself through the chaos that raged in her ears, and she wasn't even sure it was her who had said it. But the wall either could not comprehend her, or simply did not care. Black, dark orange, scarlet, a sinister dark blue. Anger, fear, pain, chaos. Cel na gobeithia chan yn cyfnewid 'r byd. The colours were all she could see now, dripping paint across her dilated pupils.

"Odette," someone far-off called, the same harsh ragged voice that had sought her yesterday. Except now it fell on her ears like the sweet melody of her saviour. With a single fluid motion that sent shock waves shuddering down her body, she twisted her body and her gaze away from the colour wall, seeking the voice in the darkness behind her. She tried to open her mouth to respond, but her larynx was locked down in chains of silence. The hypnotic power swiftly regained its sway, and she turned back, slowly, to feast upon the wealth of the colours again. It did not batter at her soul this time, it presented an array of more soothing colours; royal blue, mauve, dun, and light grey. Feelings of euphoria overwhelmed her, as if an opiate had been injected into her soul. Her head felt giddy, but she didn't pass out, she just kept drinking in the dizzying emotions.

"Odette," the ragged voice reiterated, significantly closer now. She didn't turn away from the wall this time, she didn't want to. The hues presented to her began to grow darker, but the drugged feeling didn't fade away, it was just reinforced as black, clouded grey, and dark brown raced before her eyes. She felt like she understood better now, the emotions still came, just not as fast, and filtered through a screen of delusional pleasure. Lavish colours were heaped upon her; pink, dark purple, orange, pale yellow. She stayed on her knees, but she was relaxed now, enjoying the beautiful show.

"Odette," the voice was almost right behind her now, echoing inside the room. She heard the squelching of the mud as something approached her with a shambling walk. She could hear the patchy, forced breathing of a creature in the darkness. But she felt no fear; the wall did not want her to feel fear. The thought that she was an offering for this strange creature had crossed her mind more than once, but the thought filled her with an idiotic joy. After all, if this was so it was because the wall dictated it so, and the wall had already given her so much. She kept her gaze fixed resolutely on the colours that it sprayed before her eyes, even when she felt the breathing on the back of her neck. There was a rustling behind her, and then a strange claw hand clamped down on her shoulder. In a moment, the feelings of euphoria drained away, a storm of black rushed across the wall, and Odette whirled around, screaming. The creature that stood before her, still half-concealed in the darkness, resembled a gigantic bird, shambling on two feet. But it was naked, almost unnaturally so, its grey flesh heaving back and forth in unrest. It had thin hands with five long claws in place of fingers. A huge eye-catching diamond-studded ring decorated the right index claw of its left hand. It cocked its large head to one side, surveying her intently with a round beady eye. A thin line of oozing black liquid trickled from its ashen grey beak. It wore a white doctor's coat, and the red-lined white name tag read Alexander. She took a step backwards from it and fell down, shrieking, her eyes closing for a fraction of a second.

When they opened she was sitting upright on Anna's bed, still screaming. Anna sat across the room, leaning against the wall and nursing her burned hand. She looked at Odette with a wry expression of curiosity, as Odette slapped a hand over her own mouth to halt her screaming.

"You fainted," Anna stated in a matter of fact tone.

"Oh," Odette said dully, trying to wrap her mind around what had just happened. Burning with Anna seemed like a distant memory. It slowly trickled back as she concentrated on it, and she glanced down at the angry red slash on her arm. "How long was I . . . asleep?"

Anna shrugged. "Maybe half an hour. It was awhile . . . I didn't want to wake you, I figured you needed a recovery sleep." She smiled wickedly and licked her lips again.

"You're psycho," Odette said, rubbing numbly at her forehead.

"Yeah, I know," Anna agreed cheerfully. "I can't help it, I was born that way."

CHAPTER 3

mein oberwelt

Odette's eyes flickered open to read the clock hanging above her. Five thirty. And it was Friday morning. Odette loved Fridays, mostly because she hated school, and anything that was a harbinger of doom for that institution was welcome news to her. She rolled slowly out of bed, landing on her hands and knees upon the carpet. She considered nestling herself into the warm floor, but then she pulled herself groaning to her feet. She slipped into a pair of black jeans and a graphic white t-shirt with blue butterflies fluttering across it. Dieter was nowhere to be seen downstairs, probably already gone to work; he was an insurance salesman, if Odette recalled correctly. Marie was still asleep, so Odette had the house to herself, a rare commodity. She fixed up a breakfast of thick oatmeal, drizzled with ketchup, and a glass of cola, flavoured with a small tint of vodka ferreted down from an upper cupboard. A thick fog hung outside, dampening the darkness. Odette doubted it would dissipate when the sun rose, but she didn't mind fog. It felt more comforting and protective than pure darkness, like a soft blanket with a dozen reassuring layers, stretching outwards to consume the world. She sat down at the small kitchen table to eat her slightly odd breakfast, staring fancifully out the windows above the double sink. It was still pitch outside, but she knew that dawn would come soon.

Odette decided to leave the house before Marie woke up, she could spend some time dawdling in the streets. She pulled on a thin jacket, but she didn't find the cold unbearable. It nipped slightly at her nose and her fingertips, and her breath turned into white trails of mist, but otherwise it was thoroughly comfortable. She loved breathing in crisp air, it always felt more alive than the stagnating warm variation. The fog had thinned slightly, enough to allow a few slender rays of sunlight to pierce through and dance precariously on the pavement. Odette walked slowly, she was in no rush to get anywhere in particular. Images kept dancing through the fog; mask-like faces drifting around her, fixed in expressions of horror, ringing bells swinging back and forth, a strange man in a long brown coat walking with a resolute purpose. A large barking dog made of mist ran right past her, howling its ghostly warnings into nothingness, before vanishing into the cloud's gaping maw. She whirled around as it dashed past, but it was gone before she could get a proper look at it. She turned back towards the school, hugging her jacket around her. She started to hear distant voices calling out unintelligible words, a fox hunt came trampling through the murky street, blowing horns and shouting. The yelp of dogs and the whinny of racing horses echoed against the cold concrete of the street. In the distance she heard the singular, ear-cracking sound of a gunshot. It hung in the air for a moment, unwilling to immediately depart for its distant heaven. The fox hunt disappeared into the white shadows, in frantic pursuit of their cruel sport. Moments later, a white fox came sauntering into Odette's sight. It turned and winked at her before setting off after the hapless hunters.

The fox's mischievously sparkling eyes still drifted through the corridors of Odette's mind as she sat through her morning classes, history, French literature, and civics. It was her first year in Secondary, but she still wasn't able to take school seriously. What was the point, when she was just going to end up committed in some pristine institute as an adult anyway? She had been a good student before the age of thirteen, when her hallucinations started, consuming and possessing her mind. A remarkably young age for it to begin, the doctor had said. It hadn't made her feel better.

Odette sat in the cafeteria for lunch, aimlessly picking at the unappetising food she had selected without looking. There had been no sign of Anna at all that day, but it was not unusual for her not to come to school. She just usually told Odette beforehand if she was planning on skipping out. Odette would have been worried about her, but it never crossed her mind that anything bad could happen to Anna. She was just too . . . unsinkable. Odette pushed her food away from her with a sigh. She hated fish.

"Where's your friend?" She looked up in surprise as the voice sounded right beside her. She had been too preoccupied inside her own mind to notice anyone approaching. She looked over the speaker with an expression that was far from friendly; he was a boy, obviously another Gymnasiast, wearing a red Bayern München jersey under a light blue sports jacket, with short-cut brown hair under his roguish cap. He was cute, but this didn't redeem him from the fact that he was smiling broadly, as if he had just accomplished something remarkable.

"I don't know," Odette answered curtly, after a long moment. The boy's implacable smile didn't even waver.

"She's a little frightening, isn't she?" he asked. The jocular tone he spoke with rankled under Odette's skin. What hideous gargoyle had spat up this little annoying piece of shit?

"She's my friend," Odette replied coldly. She hoped he would turn into an icicle and melt into a little bloody puddle on the floor.

"Of course," he sounded no less merry. He didn't appear to be aware of exactly how annoying he was, either that or he relished it. "My name's Bastian," he stuck out an extremely unwelcome hand. Odette stared at it for a long moment, entertaining the idea of driving her fork through his palm, before she finally succumbed and took it lightly in her fingers. He gave them a quick squeeze, his smile inexplicably broadening. "What's yours?"

"Piss off," she spat the words out as if it were poisonous. Which she sincerely hoped it was.

"Pretty name," Bastian said, sitting down across from her without so much as asking for an invitation.

"What do you want?" Odette demanded. Her eyes drifted back to her fork, lying so innocently on the table. She wondered if he would still be grinning with it driven through his eye.

"Well, your girlfriend is gone for once, so I thought I might take this opportunity to get acquainted." There was a fairly widespread rumour in school that Odette and Anna were lesbians, mostly due to Anna's extremely boyish appearance. Normally neither of them even remotely cared what the school idiots babbled about, but right now Odette wanted to execute all of them.

"She's not my . . . Jesus Christ," Odette pulled her plate back, stabbing violently at the hapless fish. She didn't even want to look at this annoying boy and his stupid smirk. What the fuck did he want anyway? "We're not . . . goddamn. Did you come over here just to piss me off?"

"No, no, no, of course not. I'm sorry," Odette glanced up at him; he was still smiling, but it was a slightly more contrite smile now. "I can be a bit of a jackass," Bastian continued. "I don't mean any harm though." Odette just scowled at him, and his grin broadened. "So what are you doing this weekend?"

"I don't know," she hissed, turning her attention back to the now-mutilated fish. She pushed her plate aside again petulantly. Why wouldn't this . . . boy just go away and leave her alone?

"No plans at all?" Bastian raised an eyebrow. "Just going to stay at home and practice witchcraft and sacrifice little animals?"

"That sounds like a typical weekend for me," Odette injected as much acid into her voice as possible.

"Good to know," Bastian's smile grew even wider, somehow. Odette hoped that his face would split in half if it expanded any further. "Well, if you ever get tired of casting horrible curses on people and sending rabbit souls to heaven, there are slightly less psychotic alternatives."

"What if I like psychotic?" Odette tilted her head tauntingly.

"I hear they have medication for that."

"I'm on it . . . didn't work."

Bastian laughed, but it was not the abrasive braying sound Odette had prepared herself for. She actually found it mildly pleasant.

"Well, if you ever change your mind," he said. "I'll be open to suggesting alternatives." For a moment his head exploded in a burst of white feathers, but then Odette blinked, and his grinning features were restored.

"I'll think about it," Odette answered, without even thinking about it. A moment later she desperately hoped that she hadn't said it in a tone that could be in any way misconstrued as inviting. She didn't want to give this little freak any light of hope, he seemed to operate well enough without it.

"Excellent," he was practically beaming as he stood up, a nauseating sight. "I have to go, or I'll be late for class," he continued, his voice dripping sunshine. All the pleasant feelings his laugh had fostered in Odette were long fled now, and she scowled at him. His laughing exit was half-shrouded in a cloud of green-tinted smoke, but she could still just make him out walking backwards through the cafeteria's double doors. The cloud hissed and disappeared, leaving droplets of green ooze crawling across the cold floor. Odette didn't look at them, she was staring with tilted head at the still swinging doors and the darkness that oscillated between them.

Odette clutched the sides of the white bathroom sink, staring at her reflection in the wide mirror. A drop of water trickled slowly towards its inevitable demise in the uncharted depths of the rapacious drain. The clean world around her was eerily silent, the walls softly filtering in the distant sounds of movement and voices. The mirror shimmered like a pond disturbed by a falling stone, distorting her reflection into a strange creature covered with cascading black mud. Glowing symbols formed and disappeared in the mudslide, too quickly for Odette to read them.

She closed her eyes to keep them from burning up in the message, she felt the dark glow scarring her pupils. When her eyelids flickered open, against her will, the mirror was restored to its former self, no trace of the transformation remaining. She felt cold sweat crawling across her skin as she stretched out a finger to touch the mirror. When her nail scraped the glass all she felt was her reflection's frigid breath on her hand. She drew it back quickly, fumbling through her purse before her fingers emerged clutching a tube of red lipstick. She raised it slowly to her throat, staring intently at the figure gazing solemnly back at her. She drew a thick red line across her jugular vein, before dropping her hand limply to her side. For a moment the figure in the mirror stood motionless. Then her eyes widened in fear as the crimson gash across her throat began to bleed, trickling down her pale skin and dripping onto her breast. Her hand shot in panic to the widening cut, before she crumpled silently to the floor. Odette watched, passive and motionless, before the creaking of the bathroom door opening disturbed her reverie. She quickly switched on the spigot and leaned down into the sink, washing the murderous smear from her throat. The thin crimson lines paled to pink in the swirling water, before disappearing into the darkness.

CHAPTER 4

voller hoffnung die tinte willst trocken

Dieter was comfortably ensconced in his armchair watching a football highlights show when Odette wearily pushed the front door of the Schiller's house open. He didn't even look up when she traipsed past, which she was grateful for. She had already received more attention that she was fond of for that day. The eager sound of the commentator's voice faded away as Odette stumbled up the stairs and shut her door behind her. She threw her books down on her bed and sighed. The walls were dripping thick black liquid, but she hardly even glanced at them, even though it cascaded down and spread across the floor, staining her beige tennis shoes. It swiftly swallowed up her footprints when she turned around and walked out of the room.

"Marie?" Odette poked her head into the Schiller's bedroom. Marie was folding laundry on the bed.

"Yes, dear?" she asked, looking up. Odette couldn't help but like her; at twenty-nine she seemed too young to be her biological mother, which made Odette feel more comfortable around her. She hated older people who were always flexing their authority. Marie was a tall woman, the same height as her husband, with dark hair that she usually kept tied up in a ponytail. She moved with lithe grace and quiet confidence, and her grey eyes were lucid with compassion.

"Can i use the phone?" Odette asked, clinging to the door post and resting her head against the wall.

"Yeah, of course," Marie answered, quickly folding up a blouse and setting it down on the bed. Odette wished she could move with that kind of precise beauty. "Who are you calling?"

"Anna. She didn't come to school today, I don't know why," Odette said, her eyes automatically following Marie's serpentine movements.

"I hope she's not sick," Marie's voice had genuine worry in it. No matter what she might think of Odette and Anna's friendship, she was not one to project negative feelings on an actual person.

"Thanks," Odette whispered shyly, ducking out of the room. She pattered down the stairs and past the still immobile Dieter, into the kitchen, where the phone hung on the wall next to the refrigerator. Anna had a cell phone, which was fortunate, Odette didn't really want to talk to either of Anna's parents. They usually made very little effort to mask their dislike of her. The phone rang three times before Anna's slightly stifled voice answered.

"Hello?"

"Hey, it's Odette," for some reason she always spoke in a whisper when talking over a telephone. She could probably have screamed and Dieter would still not have heard it.

"Oh, hey," said Anna, the natural hostility in her voice fading away. "What's up?"

"Where were you today?" Odette demanded, in more of a stage whisper now. "Some freak harassed me at lunch in the cafeteria today, I wanted to stab him."

"Did you?" Anna's voice lit up with curiosity.

"No," Odette sighed. "I didn't have a knife. I think he was hitting on me or something."

"What was his name?"

"I don't remember," Odette lied after a moment's pause. For some unknown reason she didn't want Anna hunting Bastian down and skinning him alive, even though parted of her really wanted to watch. "I tried to ignore him. He was just some idiotic boy. Anyway, where were you today?" She wished she hadn't brought up the subject of Bastian. He wasn't that cute. She scowled into the phone, the dialogue from earlier that day rolling like a film reel through her head. Bah.

"My parents had me in family therapy the entire fucking morning," Anna replied, venom creeping back into her voice. "To address my antisocial behaviour, my rebellion, and a lot of other things that I didn't really pay very much attention to. The guy was an idiot anyway. He thinks i have an Electra complex, which is the root of my rebellious behaviour. It was a gigantic fucking waste of time. It was actually significantly worse than just going to fucking school."

"That sounds bad," Odette sympathised. Her mind kept wandering back to Bastian, which was starting to annoy her. *Maybe his parents will die and that will wipe the fucking smile off his fucking face.* "I'm glad you aren't sick."

"Yeah . . . thanks," Anna said. "This was actually worse than being sick though, trust me. I'd take the black plague over having to go back into that son of a bitch's stinking little therapeutic hellhole."

"Are you going to have to go back?"

Anna's sigh was distinctly audible. "I fucking hope not. It's not really up to me though and my parents gushed about it. They thought it was great, like the drivelling idiots they are."

"Damn. That sucks." *Why could she get this stupid boy out of her head? If he comes and talks to me on Monday I'm going to stab him.*

"Yeah," Anna agreed, a hopeless note taking over her voice. "More sessions with Dr. Krasinski . . . the things my dreams are made of."

"See you tomorrow?" Odette asked.

"Yeah," Anna said slowly. "I might have to sneak out, but I will if I have to. There's no way I'm spending the weekend with my fucking parents, they've already put me through enough torture. I wish they would just leave me the fuck alone. Honestly you're lucky that yours are dead."

"Probably," Odette almost laughed. "Foster parents are pretty great, they don't even give a fuck. Well, Marie does, but it's not like she bothers me about it."

"Yeah, she's cool," Anna agreed. "Why can't more adults be like that? They're all such drooling morons."

Odette concurred in a subdued murmur, thoughts of Bastian still cascading unbidden through her mind. What's wrong with me? She kicked the wall suddenly, biting down on her lip until it bled. A small red teardrop trickled out of her mouth and down her pale chin, dripping depleted to the floor. "I'll see you tomorrow then," Odette whispered and hung up the phone as Anna launched on another hate-filled diatribe against the world. Breathe.

Sleep, as usual, came with a great level of difficulty. The rhythmic pole thumping pounded out steadily outside her door, driving sharp shafts of pain through her fragile skull. Odette tossed helplessly in her bed, desperately and fruitlessly trying to block out the terrorising noises that plagued her. She felt as if some malefic of a spirit followed her and tormented her, making her life his plaything, and the ruin of it his masterpiece. A bleeding rose drifted down from her ceiling, some strange red light illuminating it in its cherished fall from grace. Then it passed through her floor, petals fluttering around it in a cold wind, and the light disappeared, leaving her room once again blanketed in darkness. She cowered deeper into her bed, pulling the comforter over her head. It did nothing to stifle out the steady thump-thump-thump of course, but at least it shielded her eyes from whatever tricks the cruel spirit chose to play on her. Every now and then a shaft of moonlight would streak through the encircling bastions of fog and dance merrily on her floor for the duration of its short life-span.

There was no respite for her once she was swallowed up by the jaws of slumber. The spirit pursued her there, where it held sway with far greater purpose than it could ever exert in the cold light of day. The darkness swelled and faded around here, consuming and then consumed, glutted with a thousand lost souls of people forlorn. They cried out to Odette as she fled past them, their chains rattling in the wind, their cold white grins piercing the shadows that engulfed them.

"Save us, save us, goddess of mercy," they wailed mournfully, all the pain of their violent passing contained in their sepulchral voices. "Have mercy upon the lost, as they once had mercy on their fellow man."

She tried to ignore them, tripping and stumbling aimlessly through the darkness. She could see no light ahead of her nor behind, there was no glimmer of hope in this place. The floor beneath her was cracked stone, uneven and treacherous, but reminiscent of glories long dead, buried beneath the relentless sandstorm of time. She tried to feel around in the black with her hands, but all they touched was more cold air, empty and whistling. Fear gripped at her heart, crushing it beneath rapidly constricting iron bands. The ghosts kept shrieking in the darkness behind her, flickering like torches in the wind.

Then she was standing before the wall, lost in its cascading rainbow of glory. It lit up the empty room around her with its ever-changing glow, dispelling the banshees that haunted the cobwebs of her mind. Nothing had ever seemed so perfect, so flawless in its message, as this opiate of a monument. With one stroke of its paintbrush it reigned supreme in her mind, blotting everything else out in a swirl of colour and emotion. They were softer and more sensuous now, stroking her with loving fingers as they danced beautifully across her soul, lighting desire in her longing pupils. Nothing could compare with this turning wheel of fortune, painted water spilling across its rotating silver cogs, transcendent in sparkling splendour. Odette dropped to her knees, her breath echoing loud in her ears, as she let the wall take control of her heart, filling it up with the deepest and the highest of ecstasy. An endless well of emotion thrown about by a blessed earthquake to spill across the sky, hanging there like smoke until only the traces of a glorious past remained, eternal reminders of the darkened light. The key mysterious, concealed by a mist of fable and the drums of solitude. Odette just knelt there, wrapped up in downy raiment of a sky-soaked bliss, wandering with boundless curiosity in the depths of her own eyes. Paradoxes rotating in perfect circles laid down on the cobblestones of the street, each sphere holding the watery sparkle of starlight. Yellow, purple, red, they painted the walls of her soul with their gentle fingers, stroking the shining interior into a brilliant burst of colour. All she could do was sit and marvel at this beautiful subversion of her mind, dancing motes of starlight dragging away the cold chains that had encircled it.

"Odette?" She recognised Alexander's voice now, harsh and cracking against the stones. It seemed out of place in this sanctuary of endless splendour. She tried to open her lips to reply, but they seemed bound under the wall's spell. Shades of flowers spread gracefully across the wall, soft pinks and carnation reds, swelling her heart up with new tides of emotion. The slough of mud had been replaced with a soft grassy meadow, dotted with daisies and roses.

"Odette?" His ragged voice rang out again; it sounded thin in the open meadow air. Odette could hear his shuffling step as the grass bent and parted around his white-shoed feet. Can he say nothing but my name? He did not belong here, not in this place. His home was the mud and the darkness, no one belonged in this garden but the creator. It was not meant for fragile mortal eyes, lest they be consumed with it and wander shattered for eternity. Alexander's claws touched her shoulder, but they felt veiled, as if a cloth were thrown over them. Perhaps he was not here at all.

"My Lady?" he asked, his voice coloured with a note of strange worry. For the first time she noticed the reverence that coated his touch and tone. She turned her head and caught the white glimmer of his coat out of the corner of her eye. It flapped about as a stray wind caught it, warm and eddying from the south. She closed her eyes and listened to the crackling sound of the plastic blowing against itself. It was a jarring sound, but not unfamiliar enough to be frightening. She turned her head with her eyes still closed, listening more carefully until she heard the barely discernible sound of Alexander's uneven breathing.

"What do you want from me?" she asked, the rebellion that clasped her tongue finally quelled. Her tone sounded more savage than she had intended, but perhaps it was best to show aggression with this strange stalker of her dreams, this intruder into her most sacred hideaway. She was surprised at the emotions that sprang up in her heart, she felt a deep longing to punish him for his unholy trespasses.

"To worship," Alexander rasped after a long pause. The reverence hidden latent in his voice rose to the surface, dripping from his words. She could feel his head incline in respect as he stood behind her.

"Worship who?" Odette demanded, still keeping her gaze firmly fastened on the colours that were dancing at her bidding now. Pirouettes of sweeping sunshine swept across the wall, sending a shock of blinding light across the meadow.

"Our Lady of Mercy, Odette, at her Tapestry," Alexander replied, and it sounded like a prayer. His claws had slipped from her shoulder and she could hear them fold inside each other as the strange creature knelt behind her, his breath slowing down into structured timing as the waves of the wall crashed over his prostrate soul. She could feel it consuming him, wrapping him up in its all-encompassing arms just as it had her. She rose to her feet and turned to look at him; she could see a light so familiar burning in his eyes as he stared entranced at the vision that had snared her in its sweet-smelling web. She stretched out her hand slowly, shaking, until her pale fingers rested on her genuflecting acolyte's shoulder. She exhaled, almost in relief, as he remained bowed before her, before her wall. What had he called it? Her Tapestry.

"Alexander?" she spoke it as a question, but was shocked to hear how imperious her voice suddenly sounded. The strange creature raised his humbled head, the light of the Tapestry still glowing in his pupils. He didn't reply, but his manner radiated obedience. "Who are you?"

"I am Alexander von Krankenhaus, your devoted High Priest, my Lady. Never before have our people, so fervent in their worship of your Grace, been favoured beyond our wildest dreams as we are today, and always you have rained mercy and plenty upon our blessed hearts. We extend our most earnest of thanks that you have shown the kindness to descend from the stars to walk among us, in our era of most dire need. Flawless is the compunction of our esteemed Goddess."

"Dire need?" Odette asked, keeping her hand on the priest's shoulder.

"We know your duties are many, my Lady, and many people worship your beauty and grace, on this planet and others, although most of them, as the foul Bloods, pervert your holy teachings into missives for their own advancement. The humble Metropolitan people have been struck with a horrendous blight that has wasted our population, leaving the vast majority ill or dying. It is believed by many of our foremost scientists that the Dark Blight, as it is named, was engineered by the Bloods in their dark refuge to exact revenge upon my people for our prosperity and our faith. But in our hearts we have held true to your words and teachings and we have been justly rewarded with your most merciful salvation." The broad ray of hope that crept into his cracked voice was unmistakable, and a fanatical spark took hold in his eyes.

"I come here a lot," Odette said slowly, gesturing over her shoulder at the Tapestry, which continued to shimmer and sparkle, projecting its ever-changing aura of emotion across the blessed sanctuary.

"I have seen the phantom of our Goddess several times in the last few days," Alexander replied. "I cried out to you for beneficence, but now I see that your wisdom far surpasses mine and it was foolish of me to interfere in the workings of our Lady. You concentrated deeply upon the Tapestry, our greatest relic of yours which we keep housed in the most secure of locations to thwart the vile Blood saboteurs who hold nothing in respect. Your Metropolitan people have all felt your touch on the Tapestry stirring in the roots of their hearts, caressing the oil in our veins, all of which we would gladly spill in our zealous devotion to you."

"I'm not a god," Odette's brow furrowed as she tried to ponder everything the priest was saying. "I'm just a girl . . . there's nothing special about me, I can't save anyone. I'm not even good at anything."

Alexander did not respond for a moment that seemed to stretch towards eternity, and when he finally spoke, it was in the slowest of measured voices. "Perhaps you are not yet aware of the great spirit that has taken control of you, child. Do not worry, she will unveil her desires to you in time . . . hopefully in a swift passing of time. Such a thing would not be unheard of."

"What?" Odette dropped her hand from the priest's shoulder. "No . . . no, my name is Odette but I'm not a goddess or anything like that, OK? I can't help you, I just come here to look at this wall because . . . well I don't know why I come here I just end up here but I like it so I try to stay, but I can't fix your problems or heal anyone of this sickness or whatever it is. I don't even know who you are or who the Metropolitans are, I've never heard of any of it . . ."

"Peace, child," Alexander said, slowly rising to his feet and placing a clawed hand over Odette's forehead. "Do not hold fear or worry in your heart. Cherish only the most sacred of emotions so that her will may be revealed to you with all the more haste, for my people are in desperate need of her aid."

Odette drew backwards, shrinking away from his touch and shaking her head in confusion. "No . . . no . . ." she murmured. How could this happen in her sanctuary? Why wouldn't he just go away and leave her in peace? She fell down on her knees, clutching her head in her hands. Alexander folded his claws inside his white doctor's coat, watching the spectacle with passive detachment in his round bird-like eyes. Odette heard a sound ringing in her ears, and it was only after a minute that she realised it was her own screams. She felt dazed, shocked, where was her Tapestry to paint this away? She couldn't gather enough willpower to turn back to it, to beseech it for its help. It had to be able to drive this out of her mind, it could control and shape what it willed . . . but perhaps it was willing this and nothing could dispel it. She wasn't God here, the Tapestry was, it controlled her heart entirely, taking and giving as it saw fit. Surely it could hear her shrieks, the uncontrolled screaming issuing from her mind and spiralling into the roof. The meadow faded away, leaving only a small dark room, with triangular dark walls and a squelching mud floor. The Tapestry behind her darkened into a menacing storm, withdrawing its light from shining around her. Cold bursts of wind came howling from nowhere, rushing their unwelcome hands across her bare skin. Wrenching her hands down from her eyes, she looked up to see that Alexander had disappeared with the meadow. She whipped her head around frantically, but her searching eyes only saw more shadows, swirling and crowding around her. She was alone in the darkness, abandoned, desolate, stripped of the power Alexander had attempted to invest her with. She stumbled around the darkened room, falling heavily against one of the walls.

Her vision was blurred, perforated by fear, even the the pitch black seemed to swim unsteadily before her. She reached forward into the air and fell down onto her hands and knees. Her eyelids snapped shut, striving helplessly to shut out the terror that danced merrily around her. Why wouldn't it all just go away?

CHAPTER 5

mit tod ich tanzen

"With eyes wide shut I stand, wandering the world of sinful man."

Odette's eyelids fluttered open. The first thing that came into focus was the clock that hung above her. She didn't even bother to read it, since the time didn't matter anyway. It was Saturday, after all, the blessed day that all those crushing adult expectations didn't apply. She rolled her eyeballs around her sparsely decorated white room, contemplating whether or not she wanted to emerge from the comfort of her bed just yet. Sloth finally won out and she settled back down into the warmth with a contented sigh.

"Odette?"

Odette's eyes sprang open to realise she had slipped back into slumber. She looked drowsily up at Marie, who stood in her doorway. "What is it?" she asked, yawning and rubbing at her sleep-speckled eyes.

"Your friend Anna just called. She wants you to meet her at a place called L'Affliction, whatever that is."

L'Affliction was an underground club for sanguinarians; people who liked to live a fantasy vampiric lifestyle. Anna was friends with several of them and she adored them; their bloodplay fetishes, their dark gothic clothing, their pale makeup. It was never open in the day, but Odette found Anna lounging on a bench near the ominous-looking entrance to the club. She sat down next to her, gratefully accepting the cigarette and lighter that Anna offered her.

"Did you have to sneak out?" Odette asked, inhaling a long satisfying drag of nicotine.

"Yeah," Anna laughed bitterly. "They told me they wanted me to spend time with them over the weekend . . . I'd rather shoot myself, to be honest. God, they're annoying. They're gonna make me go to church with them tomorrow. I think I'm going to tell them I worship the devil. Not that it would surprise them very much, I think they're just desperately trying to get me from selling my soul. Guess what my mother asked me last night?"

"What?" Odette obliged, tapping her cigarette on the metal side of the bench. Morning dew still sparkled in the sunlight.

"She asked me if I was out walking the streets. When I asked her what she meant, she asked if I was working as a prostitute."

"Wow," Odette stared at the smoke curling softly through the air.

"You're lucky, you know. When you're an adult you're gonna end up in a lunatic asylum, but I'm going straight to prison," Anna laughed, lighting up a cigarette of her own. Odette wasn't completely sure where she got them, but she always seemed to have a large supply.

"What makes an asylum better than a prison?"

"All the fun stuff happens in asylums," Anna explained. "All the shrieking ghosts in long white bloodstained gowns live there. Prison is boring."

"We wouldn't want to miss out on shrieking ghosts," Odette giggled a little, looking up at the half-shrouded sun. Even filtered as it was, it was far too bright for her liking.

"Come on," Anna said, standing up and tugging at Odette's shirt-sleeve.

"Where are we going," Odette whined, inhaling another pleasing dose of cigarette smoke.

"I want you to meet someone," Anna answered mysteriously, pulling Odette up to her feet. "Come on."

The basement below L'Affliction was very dark, lit only by a single dust-spattered light bulb that hung precariously on naked wires from the ceiling. Cardboard boxes full of grotesque masks, costumes, and strange props were shoved against all the walls, festooned by an array of spider-webs, dead moths, and layers of dust. Odette stayed close behind Anna, who didn't seem in the slightest disconcerted by the macabre atmosphere.

"Are we suppose to be in here?" Odette whispered, accidentally stepping on the back of Anna's heel as she pressed a little too close.

"Au!" Anna hissed at her. "Yes," she said after a moment, with a scowl in her voice. "Til is cool, I know him. He'll be back here in his office, I think."

Til's office was not terribly different from the rest of the club's basement; dimly-lit, littered with stacked cardboard boxes filled with papers. Til himself sat in a green revolving chair in front of an ancient-looking computer monitor, staring up at the ceiling. He was a tall man, with long free-falling black hair down to the middle of his back and green and red tattoos covering his arms and neck. His smooth tanned face was covered in bizarre piercings; lip, nose, eyebrow, cheek. He turned his bright blue eyes on Anna as she walked boldly into the room, Odette cowering behind her was barely visible. He smiled, a fiercely predatory smile that made him seen even more menacing.

"Well if it isn't the little fetishist," he said in a smooth voice that reminded Odette of blood smeared over ice. He folded his long fingers together as he surveyed both of them, his eyes darting back and forth, hawk-like. "And what can Til do for Anna today?"

"Well," Anna answered, her eyes wandering teasingly around the room. "My friend here was curious about some things she hasn't had the pleasure to experience yet, and it's a boring Saturday afternoon, so I wondered if you might be interested in showing us some fun."

"No I wasn't," Odette interjected swiftly, in a desperate whisper, as Til leaned back in his chair, the predatory grin spreading wider.

"Does your friend have a name?" The tall man asked, lazily casting his gaze over Odette, who cowered further behind Anna.

"Odette," Anna answered, as the named silently shook her head. Til laughed outright at this, and Odette's pale cheeks blushed a deep red.

"Well, Odette," said Til, the pucker of laughter still on his cheeks. "How about some diacetyl morphine? Calms the nerves . . . you look a little tense."

Odette had the terrible sensation that both Anna and this tall stranger were playing games with her, but there was nothing she could do about it. She weakly nodded her head as Anna elbowed her in the ribs, a little sharper than she thought was necessary. Anna's face seemed a great deal brighter than usual. Til disappeared suddenly through an open doorway in the back of the room, leaving the room feeling vacant and somehow more grey.

"What the fuck is going on, Anna?" Odette hissed savagely, pinching her friend on the arm.

"Relax, shit," Anna seemed very pleased with the whole situation. "It's fun, you'll like it. Trust me."

Til reappeared after a couple of minutes, with a syringe half-concealed in his left hand. "Tie her off," he said to Anna, tossing her a thin red ribbon.

"Sit down," Anna commanded, guiding Odette into Til's vacant chair. "Give me your arm."

Til came circling around Anna as she tied the ribbon tight around Odette's forearm. "You have beautiful veins," the tall man whispered, running his fingers down Odette's pale skin. "Little prick," he continued, with a sarcastic smile, and a moment later plunged the needle point into one of Odette's coursing blue life-lines.

The Tapestry seemed to find a strange symmetry in the chaos that beset it, ordering the bright exploding colours into obedient little soldiers of mimicry, all streaming together towards their eternal goal. Odette's head ached as she stared at it, the clash of two worlds and their bitter resentment towards the master. She closed her eyes to shut out the dizzying display, but the Tapestry could paint on the back of her eyelids as well, and soon it flooded her mind with a fresh dose of wild control. A thousand colours all coming at once, too quickly for her mind to even process them before they disappeared into the hungering ground. She wanted to sink into the mud and be consumed like just another colour, but the devouring throat just spat her out again.

"Child?" She whirled around as she heard Alexander's hoarse voice in the darkness behind her, but he was nowhere to be seen. Then she saw a faint glimmer of white standing out like a silhouette in the crushing layers of pitch black. Yytiasa luhja. It came closer, gradually evolving into Alexander's medical coat, sheathing his repulsive shambling body.

"Ah, there you are," he said, cocking his head to the side and surveying her with a gigantic beaded eye. Odette just stared at him, recognition registering in her mind but not in her body. She felt the overwhelming urge to flee, but she managed to arrest the instinctual reaction with a calming thought. Nerves exploded like a small barrage of rockets, but she swallowed deeply and stood still.

"I was wondering where you had gone," Alexander rasped, an expression that might have been a smile forming on his twisted beak. "Come with me, sacred child," he waved his long claws towards the darkness as he turned his back on her and began shambling slowly away. For a moment Odette stood rooted to the ground, ensnared by some frozen colossus. Then she started trudging slowly through the mud in obedient pursuit. The Tapestry, as powerful and luminescent as it was, did not take long to disappear into the folds of darkness that encircled them with such predatory power. The room stretched on much further then Odette had initially thought, and the two walls stretching forth from the Tapestry drew closer and closer together, creating a claustrophobic hallway. Mud squelched and spat beneath Odette's timid steps, staining her white shoes with their brown paintings. After what seemed like hours travelling behind Alexander's oddly sloped back, a pinprick of light appeared in the darkness ahead; searing white light that hurt the eyes to look upon.

When they drew closer Odette saw that it was a keyhole in a huge black-steel door, engraved with many dark green images and symbols that she did not understand. Alexander snuffed out the light for a moment as he inserted a plaster key into the hole and turned it with a hiss. The door parted jaggedly in the middle, half of it sinking slowly into the floor and the other half retracting into the ceiling. The unhindered light that blasted through blinded Odette, and she clasped her hands over her eyes to relieve them some of the agony.

"A thousand pardons, milady," Alexander apologised contritely. "You look upon your beacon of light in an ever-darkening world. It can be . . . unsettling to an unaccustomed mortal eye." Odette peeked through a crack in her fingers at what lay beyond the Tapestry room, but for a long moment all she could see was more blinding white. Slowly objects began to detach from each other and become oblique in her perception; a long railing running along the edge of a walkway. Beyond it, far in the distance, she could make out many small black dots speckling the flawless beauty of the place, but she could not distinguish what they were. She accepted Alexander's graciously extended claw and allowed him to lead her out onto the walkway. Her eyes became more accustomed to the brightness and she saw that the objects stretched out below them were beds, thousands and thousands of beds, and in each one of them rested a small dark figure. A few figures cloaked all in white, wearing white gas masks, wound their way between the rows of beds, checking the various beeping machines and adjusting wires and needles.

"Welcome to the Grand Metropolitan Hospital," Alexander proclaimed proudly. "We continue to serve you with all the diligence and all the passion of our combined race. We have created a temple to you unparalleled in the ages, despite the horrors that beset our people at every corner. It is our vision to serve."

"What's wrong with all of them?" Odette asked, almost in a daze from the overpowering brightness. She stared, trance-like, out over the ocean of sickbeds. She could see a thick dark liquid oozing out from between the bedridden creature's beaks.

"The Dark Blight," Alexander's tone was ominous, the expression on his alien face grave. "Our best scientists have thus far been unable to explain it or provide a cure. All we can do is delay the inevitable end, and strive to make these poor creatures comfortable in their final days. They tell me that in time we will overcome it, but I know that time is not a commodity my people are wealthy in. If left unchecked, this disease will render us extinct in a matter of months. That is why I am caught with such delight that our Lady of Mercy, our saviour, has blessed us with her divine presence."

"What does it do?" Odette felt pity swelling up in her heart as she looked down at the hacking, tormented creatures.

"It corrupts the very oil in our veins and then floods our stomachs with it, so that it comes up with every cough and breath. Our black veins become distorted, angry, and the body suffers from chills and intense pain. Ultimately the death is essentially equivalent to being drowned from the inside, and it is slow, drawn-out. Some among us believe it is a curse, others a mischance, still others that it is an unholy attack upon our devoted people by our ancient enemies."

"How long can someone live after contracting it?" Odette asked breathlessly, leaning against the railing for support. She felt the air being stripped from her body, something heavy pushing down on her, oppressing her.

"Two weeks at most," Alexander folded his hands together in front of him. "It is a ruthless contagion, it effected over half our population in the first three days before we even had an idea of what we were dealing with. Already there are not enough healthy to care for the vast numbers of sick, and soon there will be none left at all."

"I . . . I can't fix this," Odette said, as the overwhelming feelings continued to sweep over her. "I don't know what to do."

"I know child," Alexander said gently, placing a soothing hand on her shoulder. "But in time . . . our salvation rests in your hands alone."

CHAPTER 6

unheilige entweihung

It was late when Odette quietly pushed open the Schiller's front door, and began to creep, mouse-like, to the staircase. She wasn't exactly sure of the time, but she was sure it was significantly later than she was suppose to be out, unaccounted for. She heard no noises in the house as her hand touched the black wooden bannister, and she fervently hoped that the Schiller's had gone to bed. At least she wouldn't have to deal with any lectures tonight, while she was tired. Such things were far better put off 'til mornings. The house was darkened, another good sign. Dieter's favourite chair in front of the TV empty. Excellent. Odette began her ascension of the staircase, carefully placing each footstep for the minimum amount of disturbance, peering quizzically at the hall above. When she reached the top she crept into her room to retrieve her night-gown, and then into the bathroom. If the Schillers were firmly asleep, there could be no harm in taking a much needed shower.

She loved the feel of warm water coursing over her naked skin. It was deeply soothing, peaceful, aromatic. Steam rose around her body as she closed her eyes and enjoyed the luscious massage of the dozens of little waterspouts striking her. She heard the dripping shower curtain pushed aside, the plastic rings rattling against the metal pipe, half a second before a strong hand grabbed at her body. She turned, blinded by the water spraying in her eyes, and tried to scream before another hand clamped over her mouth. She tried to struggle in vain, the dark figure was far superior in strength. He shifted his hand from her mouth to her jugular vein and dragged her out of the shower by her throat and arm.

She struggled to breathe, his tight fingers constricted her airflow to almost nothing as he whirled her around and pushed her up against the wall. She could still hear the water spraying, a drumming sound now as it fell, unfulfilled, to the shower floor. He pushed the back of her head into the wall, drowning out her sight as water still trickled from her ears, intermingled with hot tears of panic. She gasped as he released her throat, and then again, louder, as he entered her. It was scorching, ripping, painful. She wanted to scream, but her lungs gave out as he held her ruthlessly against the wall in an iron grip and pushed deeper, over and over. He held her wrists behind her in one hand, so hard she felt they might shatter, and kept her head pushed into the wall with his other hand. She heard him grunting in satisfaction as he kept at his bestial pursuit, harder and harder. He didn't say a word, but she felt too frightened to scream. Terror gripped her body, freezing her throat, freezing her muscles, a petrified deer in the headlights of a truck. Her eyes were frozen too, wide open in shock, tears rushing madly down her cheeks, unfettered and unheeded. She felt more helpless than she ever had before. Pain shot through her body, her stomach, her wrists, her legs. Everything felt as if it were burning up, a fire raging unchecked on her flesh. She didn't know how long it was until he released her, it felt like an eternity. When the iron grip faded away, she collapsed heavily to the floor, clawing helplessly at the wall. She heard him walking around, behind her, nonchalantly turning off the shower, then grabbing a towel and turning out the bathroom light.

She heard his steps fade away and the door to his bedroom close, but it felt filtered through a fog. Tears stung at her eyes, and she felt too frightened to even move. Half-blinded she tilted her head to look down, and saw blood trickling down her legs. Minutes ticked away as she lay breathless on the floor, trying to collect what was left of her broken soul. Her body ached, she held her wrists up before her tear-flooded eyes and saw that they were bruised, ugly black and dark purple marks were already starting to form on her pale skin. Mustering the last of her strength, she pulled herself to her feet by grabbing at the towel rack. She stood unsteadily on her feet, leaning heavily against the wall. Clinging to it, she stumbled to the door. She fell to her knees in the hallway, unable to walk any further. She crawled slowly into her bedroom, a pounding pain drilling at the front of her head. She made it to the middle of her room before she collapsed, gasping, on the carpet.

She lay and stared at the base of the wall, barely able to make it out in the darkness. The pain in her skull continued to increase, and soon it was drowning out the rest of her agony. She stretched a hand out to her bed, her arm crawling across the floor, but she couldn't gather the strength to do anything else. Slowly a merciful darkness encapsulated her, the only thing that could eliminate the pain. The last thing her stinging eyes saw before it took her completely was a white feather drifting down from her roof.

The rain pours down through the veil of night
Dark creatures flee, obscured from sight
With blue eyes and flashing fangs they prowl
Slashing the darkness with their chilling howl
The smell of blood carries on the soft breeze
Spattered with water to different degrees
Soaked fur shaken against a tall ash tree
Drenched frozen jaws snap down on what they see
A million droplets through the shadows coursing
One in a thousand but still I hear the red sing
The pack of man is entitled to crimson bliss
Gone into the night before it's seen amiss
The thrill of the hunt coursing through living veins
And all that's left is the scattered scarlet stains

Odette found herself standing in the middle of a reeking bog. She was surrounded by trees; twisted mangroves with jutting roots, weeping willows hanging protectively over her, all of them covered in vines and moss. The soft yellow ground was spongy and soft, dotted with pools of muddy water and thick peat. She was still naked, but the air was warm. She pushed aside branches that scratched at her skin as she began to slowly pick her way through the marsh. She didn't really know where she was going, but she didn't want to just stand still. It stank, the whole place seemed ingrained with a foul odour that reminded her of death. The only sounds were the croaking of bullfrogs and the soft hum of the little water striders that skimmed above the pool surfaces. Odette listened intently for other noises, but nothing assailed her ears. She felt a vague sense of fear, she wasn't sure where it came from. Something felt wrong in the back of her mind, like something was bleeding and wouldn't stop. A root grabbed at her ankle and tripped her, sending her falling to the squishy ground. She got up slowly, trying to pull mud off her skin. It hadn't hurt much, but it made her feel even more insecure. Something was very wrong.

After what felt like hours in the dark swamp, she pushed through a thick skein of thorny vines, and found herself in a wide opening. Swamp-grass jutted up from the soft dun ground, and the smell of death struck her with new force. But she ignored it, what drew her attention was a small object standing at the far end of the clearing. It was a grey stone birdbath, with four hideous gargoyle heads sculpted on each side of its base. There was gothic lettering around the rim, but she couldn't make out what it said. Green moss grew all up the base, partially hiding each of the gargoyle heads. Odette slowly moved closer to it. Some sort of strange attractive power radiated from it. For some reason she was reminded of the Tapestry, and when she saw the water in the basin she lost her breath for a moment. It was pitch black, darker than anything she had ever seen, so impenetrable to vision that it looked as deep as an ocean.

She whirled around as she heard something crashing through the swamp towards her. A savage snarl rent the air in half as a huge furred body came crashing through the thick tangle of vines, ripping them to shreds. The thing was so bright it almost glowed, a rich sapphire colour that sparkled in the dull atmosphere of the bog. Its huge pearly fangs snapped in the air, glinting with razor sharpness. Each speck of foam that flew from its roaring maw floated gently in the air, silhouetted against the darkness. Odette screamed and threw herself to the ground, but the massive creature was on her in seconds, huge claws ripping through her naked flesh. She could feel the deadly fangs at her throat as she was lifted up into the air, struggling helplessly. Suddenly it dropped her and she fell to the ground, bleeding from three deep gashes across her side. Bright tears trickled down her face as pain shot through her body. It took her a moment to realise the creature was staring down at her through narrowed pitch black eyes, reminiscent of the water in the basin. They glowed with a strange light as they looked her up and down. The creature was massive, towering above her on its hind legs. It stood at least three meters tall. Its head was long and narrow, with huge pointed ears that turned this way and that, as if assessing every sound. It dropped down to all fours, flaring nostrils sniffing Odette's shivering body. She realised that it was a giant wolf, massively muscular, its bushy tail held straight out behind it. Its shoulders and chest were covered with black tattoos; wavy flowing lines and a strange three-pointed symbol.

"Who are you?" its voice radiated strength, ringing as clear as a cathedral bell. Odette opened her mouth, but no sounds came out. Her whole body shook with fear and pain, and tears were streaming unfettered down her cheeks now, splashing onto the spongy ground. The wolf took a step back, the ruthless expression in its eyes softening.

"Tell me how a small human girl came upon the Pool of Her Soul," it spoke again, dropping its hard interrogative tone for a gentler one.

"I don't know," Odette finally managed to force words out between her desperate gasps for air. Suddenly everything came out in a panicked rush. "I was lost in the swamp. Please don't eat me, I don't know where I am. I was just wandering around and I walked into this clearing and I saw the birdbath and I just went to look at it, I wasn't going to touch it or anything. Please don't kill me."

The wolf's face took on an expression that might have been a smile. "I don't eat little girls. I prefer . . . tougher meat." He seemed to cough repeatedly, and Odette realised he was laughing. Her hand dropped trembling to the cuts in her side. Blood ran around her fingers, staining them and flowing under her fingernails. Her head began to swim as dark drops of blood spattered on the soft yellow ground. Her stomach felt sick and there was a loud buzzing in her ears, drowning out the wolf's voice. A black tunnel started to expand and contract before her eyes, threatening to swallow her up.

"I am afraid that I am not permitted to allow you to live. No one may look upon the Pool of Her Soul and live to report its location to those who seek its corruption." Odette couldn't hear the words but she could see the solemnity in his eyes and she shrank automatically away from his claws.

"I am sorry I caused you pain," the wolf continued, stalking over to stand above Odette. "Sleep now, unfortunate little one."

Odette shrieked and shut her eyes as the wolf's fangs came ripping down on her throat. For a second she could feel his breath in her face and the soft fur and wind-sharpened canines caressing her throat. Then she woke up screaming in the middle of her bedroom, lying in a pool of blood. She looked around frantically for the great blue wolf, but all she saw was the familiar four brown walls. Her hands flew to her throat and her side, but they were smooth and unmarred. The blood that she lay in was trickling from between her legs. She tried to stand, but her legs buckled under her and she collapsed into a seated position on the floor, gasping for air. Her head was still swimming, confused, disoriented; she knew something was escaping her but she couldn't pin a finger on it. She stumbled into the bathroom to get a towel to clean herself. The house was deathly quiet, she couldn't even hear so much as the rustle of soft movement. Blood dripped onto the floor tiles, spatters of dark red marring the white floor. A feeling of terror swept over her as she stood in the middle of the bathroom and she snatched a pale green towel and ran back into her room, collapsing panting on the floor. She grabbed at her throat again, almost expecting to find the creature's fang marks indented in her skin, as if he had just assaulted her in the bathroom.

She felt as if somebody were strangling her, leaving her choking on the air that was meant to give her life. She looked down at her torn bleeding skin, dabbing at it gently with the towel. Confusion reigned in her already chaotic mind, nothing made sense. Reality was rent asunder, now everything was scampering loose, rollicking joyfully across the burning hallways of her brain. The world spun around her, a sickening feeling rose in her stomach, and she vomited on the carpet. Something pounded on the inside of her skull, as if it was being squeezed by iron fingers, tighter and tighter. Cold sweat trickled down her face, cooling her feverish skin and then dropping softly to the floor. She tried to hold herself still, hold her world still, for just a moment. She gripped the carpet in her fingers, grabbing at as if it could somehow pull her from the danger she was up to her neck in. Gradually, the world slowed down, the kaleidoscopic spinning stopped, leaving only her, a panting girl on the floor. She sat up and wrapped the bloody towel around her body, shivering and looking around. The same four walls, the same carpet, the same bed. Everything looked so shockingly familiar, but it was like a new coat of paint had been sprayed over all of it. Odette struggled to her feet, stumbling a few steps, then falling into her bed. She closed her eyes, trying to shut everything out, even the little nagging voice at the base of her brain. Finally it fell quiet, and the world drifted away.

CHAPTER 7

bienenmarz

Clocks tick away, la la, a merry tune of dancing birds on the world clouded by the wretched bile of ants. La la la la, sing the ants . . .

The world did not come drifting back so much as rushing like a bullet train, shocking Odette back into consciousness with the force of its impact. For a long moment she could hear nothing, then a calm, precise voice chanting words fell on her ears.

My medicines stick inside my throat,
Water rushing across my teeth,
Power invested in a smooth white coat,
Around my neck a poisoned wreath,
White and foul I crack them open,
Tasting all the laughing decay,
Thrusting in my deepest den,
Eating up my darkest day,
After all the mobs don't care,

Burning witches at the stake,
All the circling faces stare,
Drowning witches in the lake,
Death is their closest friend,
When they all united stand,
But I laugh for in the end,
I will die by my own hand . . .

Odette's eyes snapped open suddenly, but she was alone in her bedroom. She scrambled hastily to her feet, a sharp jolt of pain stabbing through her head. Dried blood felt heavy on her skin, weighing down her soul with the force of an unwelcome memory. She staggered for a moment, her head swimming around the room. She regained her equilibrium just before she fell into the wall.

She poked her head carefully out into the hallway, but there was no sign of the Schillers. She crept into the bathroom, she felt a compelling need to wash away all the evidence of what had happened the night before, whatever it had been. Perhaps it had been nothing but another ugly dream. She prayed to whatever cruel gods were drifting out there that this was true, as she twisted the bathroom spigot. A rush of fear swept across her soul as the water splashed against the smooth white tiles of the shower floor and she looked around desperately, waiting for something to come rushing out of the darkness towards her. Minutes dragged on as she stood frozen, cleansing water rushing across her skin, banishing the blood, but still nothing came. She barely felt as if she could blink, in that fraction of night she would be even more vulnerable than she already was. The water felt unclean on her flesh, everything felt unclean; the air, the floor, the wall, her mind. It was all caked in dirt and filth, she wished she was suspended in a void of nothing so that none of it could touch her. She kept having to remind herself to breathe, it didn't seem to come naturally any more. Water poured into her eyes and lips, stinging the soft surfaces, but she barely even noticed. The darkness displayed a rank disregard for the bathroom light, consuming her and encircling her in mysterious talons. She felt trapped, the fear in the shower grew and grew, but she was terrified of stepping outside the curtain, and she still didn't feel clean. Where was her tapestry now to carry her off into a world of sparkling colour? She tried to conjure it on the plain bathroom wall, but the drab beige steadfastly refused to change. She wanted to close her eyes to see if it would come rushing out of the darkness, but she was too frightened to.

She finally dragged herself out of the shower. She was still dripping wet when she pulled on her clothes, she couldn't stand feeling naked and exposed. She went back into her room and sat on the bed, trying to summon the nerve to descend the stairs and face the Schillers. She barely even knew why she was so frightened, but she desperately hoped that they wouldn't be at home.

"Odette?" She jumped in terror at the sound of Marie's voice echoing up the stairs. "Do you want to come down and get some breakfast?"

"OK," she whispered to herself, wrapping her arms protectively around her body.

"Odette?" Marie called again. "Did you go back to bed?"

Odette poked her head out of her bedroom door. Marie stood, smiling, at the bottom of the stairs. Her smile faded away as she saw the raw panic running rampant in Odette's eyes as the girl's gaze shot wildly around the staircase and the hall.

"Sweetie, are you alright?" Marie asked. "Do you want to come down and talk?"

Odette nodded mutely, slowly emerging from the protective covers of her room. The left side of her shirt was soaked through with water, but she didn't even notice its sodden flapping against her side. Her bare feet took each step with frightened timidity, new fear shooting through her body every time her skin contacted the cold floor. Every step brought her closer to the gaping maws that awaited her below, so sure, so patient, so absolutely carnivorous. Marie put an arm around her shoulder when she reached the bottom, guiding her gently into the kitchen. Her eyes darted nervously around the room, but there was no sign of Dieter, not in his favourite chair, not at the kitchen table. Part of the weight seemed to flee from her soul when she realised that he was not home, for whatever blessed reason. She stared at the table like a dead thing as Marie sat her down before it. A bouquet of yellow flowers sat in a clear green vase of water in the centre of the table, watchfully guarding over the entire arrangement. Odette couldn't smell them. Marie put a plate in front of her, brötchen and a slice of cheese, before taking a seat herself. Odette looked up at her numbly, surprised to see an expression of worry colouring Marie's eyes.

"Is there anything you want to talk about, Odette?" She asked, her hands folded passively in her lap. Odette almost opened her mouth to allow the entire sordid story to pour forth, but some unknown chains kept her lips fastened shut. She didn't know if she could trust Marie.

He was her husband, after all. So, instead, she just mutely shook her head and stared down at her plate. The very thought of eating made her want to vomit.

"Alright . . ." Marie sounded far from convinced, but she knew the best approach was not to hound at Odette's heels. "Do you want me to take you to your football game today?" Fuck. She had forgotten about that. Anna always laughed at her for playing football, but there was something about it that she deeply enjoyed.

"I can walk," Odette whispered, picking with disinterest at her breakfast. "It's not too far off."

"I can take you," Marie insisted with a smile. "Dieter went to church with his parents today and I've nothing to do."

Odette just nodded. She didn't feel as if she had the energy to argue anything today. She definitely didn't have enough energy to play a fucking football game.

She didn't feel much more energetic by fourteen hundred, which was the time of the game. The fog-shrouded sky, pregnant with rain, didn't help improve her mood. She stared off into nothing, mindlessly performing all the pre-game stretches. Marie had stayed to watch the game, which would normally have annoyed Odette, but today she couldn't even seem to focus on it. She couldn't focus on anything, a fragmented reality cleverly eluding her fragile grasp.

"Come on, Odette," Mrs. Biewer called cheerfully, brandishing her marker board. Mrs. Biewer was the team's trainer, a short athletic blonde woman imbued with an infectious happiness. Odette trotted obediently over to join the huddle of red-shirted girls surrounding the trainer as she laid out her master plans for the destruction of the opposition.

The whistle blew, and the rain started soon after, dispelling most of Odette's disassociation. This was why she liked this game, she didn't have to think about other things, she could focus all her attention on a spinning white ball whistling across wet grass. She was a left-back, dutifully peddling up and down the side of the field, feeding in crosses to Hilde, the tall blonde striker at the spear's point. She enjoyed playing in the rain, it made concentration even more vital. The blinding torrent, the slippery field. Fatima, a small Turkish girl who played on the left wing, scored the first goal with a free kick near the edge of the box. Half time came shortly afterwards, with no stoppage to the downpour.

"Good job, girls," Mrs. Biewer enthused, scribbling unknown patterns down on her marker board. She let loose a long string of sunshine-choked orders that Odette didn't really pay attention to, staring off at ghosts in the mist.

The whistle blew again, but this time the referee was trotting over to Odette brandishing a yellow card in her right hand. "She got the ball," Hilde shouted, in the referee's face as usual, as Odette just turned and trotted away. Mrs. Biewer managed to call off Hilde before she received a card herself. "It's bullshit," she shouted at the trainer, ignoring the calming words.

The game didn't last much longer, ending 1-0. Odette hugged Fatima, her left-sided colleague. They usually won, but it was still worth celebrating.

"How was your game?" Anna passed Odette a cigarette, sheltered from the rain by a black umbrella. Odette glanced at her friend cautiously, expecting the typical laughing derision. Anna was against anything she viewed as socially acceptable behaviour, and football was definitely high on that list.

"We won," Odette finally answered, in a quiet voice.

"Cool," Anna actually smiled. Odette was slightly taken aback, but she didn't say anything. She silently watched two robins battling each other in the rain-soaked street, puffing taciturnly at the cigarette. They finally disappeared in a puddle of feathers and blood, rapidly washed away by the sheeting downpour. She almost asked Anna if she saw them, but decided it was probably best not to.

"I like the rain," she said wistfully instead.

"Why?" Anna asked, throwing a cigarette stub into the street.

"Its clean."

CHAPTER 8

alles gute zum blutige geburtstag

Here she was, back in the bathroom mirror, as blood trickled slowly down her pale arm. Shit. She covered the cut with toilet paper, wincing as the soft white sheet rapidly reddened and disintegrated. She had to go to school soon, she couldn't have an open bleeding wound.

"I'm so fucking stupid," she muttered under her breath, tossing the destroyed sheet of toilet paper into the trash can. Hopefully Marie didn't find it. Something told her Dieter wouldn't care. Goddammit. She stuffed the washed knife, a meat-carving tool pilfered from the kitchen, into her book bag. She would have to return it to its drawer before she left for school. She looked back at the livid cut on her arm, glowing red with suppressed fury. Tears started to trickle down her cheeks, but not from the pain, she was hardened to that. She angrily brushed them away, swearing under her breath. She tied a wash cloth around the wound and then went back into her room and pulled on a long-sleeved shirt. At least nobody would ask her about it then.

The first part of the day seemed to pass in a seamless haze. Anna had walked silently with her to school, a journey disrupted by a constant stream of hallucinations that Odette tried her best to ignore. Screaming people, barking dogs, zombies staggering mindlessly across her path. Classes were soaked with all their usual dullness, but Odette did her best to concentrate. For the first time she had no desire to let her mind wander, she was mortally afraid of what it might happen across. The cut on her upper arm stung, a constant distraction, but she did her best to ignore that to. Nothing seemed right today, like the whole world was shifted slightly out of place. Odette read strange things in the faces of students, of teachers, a predatory glance, a leering lustful grimace. She would always look away quickly, and when she peeked back at the offender they would be staring off at something else. She tried to tell herself she was imagining it, like she imagined everything, but the little voices whispering in the back of her head insisted that something different was going on now. It wasn't as if she had ever trusted these people, but now she wanted to flee from them screaming. Just to run into more of them. She buried her head hopelessly in her desk, wishing fervently that some comforting darkness would take her away from all of it, but it never did. The fucking perphenazine was working too well, at the worst time.

Odette sat silently next to Anna in the cafeteria, staring numbly at the food in front of her. She still felt an overwhelming urge to just get up and run away. The only thing that stopped her was that she had no idea where to run to.

"Hey, Odette," a familiar voice said from across the table. Sunshine boy. She looked up to see Bastian cheerfully perched in a chair directly across from her.

"Who the fuck are you?" Anna demanded, in a tone suggesting imminent violence.

"I was talking to Odette on Friday," Bastian answered, darting a quick smile in Anna's direction.

"Well, she doesn't want to talk to you now, asshole," Anna spat. "Get the fuck out."

"No, he can stay," Odette contradicted her quietly, completely unsure of herself. Anna stared at her with a shocked look on her face as Bastian's smile spread even further.

"How was your weekend?" The boy asked, beginning the process of rapidly demolishing his lunch.

"Pretty terrible," Odette answered truthfully, refusing to look up from her plate. Anna's face was still frozen in shock.

"I'm sorry," he sounded somewhat genuine, but Odette was sure it was a façade. Nobody was really genuine. He paused for a moment, before continuing. "Wanna go out tonight?"

Odette could feel Anna's piercing eyes drilling holes in her. "I can't tonight . . ." she answered slowly, hoping that Anna wouldn't skin her alive. "And I have football practice on Tuesday. I can Wednesday night."

"So is that a yes?" His voice sounded hopeful.

"No, it's not a fucking yes," Anna interjected rapidly. "Why don't you just leave her the fuck alone, prick?"

"Yeah," Odette still spoke slowly. She felt like she was wading through darkness. It probably didn't fucking matter anyway. "Sure."

"Cool," Bastian smiled. "I'll see you later then, OK?"

"OK," Odette mumbled, as the boy departed with his empty plate.

"What the fuck was that?" Anna whirled on her, her voice filled with screaming tension.

"Uh, a date, I guess," Odette picked aimlessly at a piece of bread with her fork.

"God . . ." Anna was almost choking with anger. "You know what he wants? Fucking. And then probably to make fun of you. We're freaks, Odette. Normal boys don't ask out freaks, OK? He wants to make a fucking mockery of you and pop your sweet little cherry."

"Its already been destroyed," Odette murmured under her breath. "The juice is running all over the place."

"What did you say?" Anna demanded, still furious.

"Nothing," Odette replied, leaning over the table and clasping her hands over the back of her head. She didn't want to leave the darkness, it felt too safe.

"No, what did you fucking say?" Anna pressed. Odette just sat quietly, staring down at the dark claustrophobic space. "Odette?"

Everything felt so small, almost like a tiny room, created by the warm walls of her skin. Dark and warm and safe.

"I'm not going to let someone do that to you," Anna continued stonily. "Not a fucking chance in fucking hell. Listen to me, Odette, what's wrong? Don't bend over for some asshole just because he has the fucking nerve to harass you, OK? Do you want me to poison him for you?"

"No," Odette murmured. She didn't realise she had started crying until she looked up into Anna's eyes. "Maybe he's not all that bad, you know?"

"OK, what the hell is wrong?" Anna's voice was gentler. "Something isn't right here. What the hell is going on?"

"Nothing. Everything is fine," Odette looked back down at the table, unwilling to lie to Anna's face.

"You can tell me anything, you know that, right?" Anna's tone had transformed into one of bleeding concern. "Odette?"

"Yeah, I know," she responded, after a long moment of silence. "I'm fine, really. Just believe me, OK?"

"OK," Anna said. She didn't sound convinced.

Odette had lost count of the number of times she had been perched on Stefani's little blue couch, reading the titles of the books in her glass bookcase. There was a green and blue glass butterfly perched next to the computer on her desk, that was new. Maybe she had bought it over the weekend.

"How are we doing today, Odette?" The tall therapist asked, producing her pen and notepad. She was wearing glasses today. She probably lost her contacts in the pile of papers she writes.

"I'm fine," Odette shrugged noncommittally. She seriously doubted Stefani cared. Well, actually she does. She's paid to care.

"Have you been having any dreams that you would like to talk about?"

Odette shook her head wordlessly. She absolutely didn't want to talk about them. Not with anyone, not even Anna. Definitely not with Stefani.

"And what about self-harm?"

"I cut myself this morning," Odette blurted out, before she even realised what she was saying. Fuck.

"Why did you do that?"

"I . . . I . . ." Odette knew exactly why she had done it, but she had no idea how to explain it. "I haven't been feeling safe."

"From yourself or from something else?" Could she sound any colder?

"Something else," she wanted to just tell her everything, like she had with Marie. This woman wasn't Dieter's wife after all. But she had never trusted Stefani, and this felt so dirty, so personal. She couldn't force the words out of her lips.

"What is it that's making you feel unsafe, Odette? Is it something you've been seeing, something you've been feeling?" Such pat questions.

"I'm not sure," Odette mumbled pathetically, looking down at her hands. Fuck, fuck, fuck, fuck.

"I'm going to have to call Marie and tell her about the cutting, Odette," Stefani said.

"OK." So?

"We can't make you stop doing this, it's important that you want to quit on your own."

"I definitely want to quit," Odette answered. Everything.

"That's excellent," Stefani smiled. "Cutting is an addiction, Odette, but it becomes a lot easier to stop when you utilise other coping skills. What do you think you could do to distract yourself or make yourself feel better when you feel the urge to cut or hurt yourself?"

"I'm not sure."

"What about music? Many people find solace and comfort in that."

"I guess that could work," Odette didn't sound convinced. Most of the music she listened to encouraged that sort of behaviour.

"Another thing you can do when you feel like self-harming is put an ice cube in your hand and squeeze it really hard. Its very effective, and a good tool to use when you first start trying to quit."

"OK," Odette answered quietly. She wondered how much Anna would laugh at that.

"Will you promise me that next time you feel like hurting yourself you will do that or talk to Marie or me? You can call me anytime. We could work through the negative things you're feeling, and it will be much better than just impulsively hurting yourself."

"OK," Odette felt numb. "I promise." Anna would laugh so much.

"Will you make a list for me before Thursday of things you feel might help you when you're feeling the urge to cut? I think it would be really beneficial."

Odette nodded wordlessly. Whatever was expected of her. She just wanted to lie down and die, but she wasn't about to tell Stefani that.

"What about the thumping? Has it been disturbing your sleep too badly? Perhaps we should look at changing your sleep medication."

Fucking thumping. Odette shook her head. "No, it hasn't been bothering me the last couple of nights." Not true, but she didn't want to have to take more drugs. She hated goddamn pills.

"Well, that's good," Stefani almost sounded disappointed. What a fucking circus.

Circus?

CHAPTER 9

dunkelheit überall

Odette collapsed into her bed, listening to the sounds of Dieter and Marie going into their room. The darkness was restful to her tired eyes, like a smooth aroma of vision. She let her eyelids flicker shut, trying to ignore the rhythmic thumping that began like clockwork outside her door. A feeling of uneasiness swept over her, and her eyes snapped open, surveying the shadows that swirled around her. But the room was still empty, although a new hint of moonlight shone through the window and played on the floor. She let her eyelids flutter shut again, safe in her feelings of solitude. The only sounds that broke the dead silence were the distant rustling of the Schillers in their bedroom. The world faded away slowly, as if it were being poured through a funnel, hypnotic sugar trickling grain by grain across a red plastic surface.

The darkness that lurked behind her eyelids seemed somehow less sinister, less pregnant with fear, than the darkness that dwelt in the quiet emptiness of her bedroom.

It was warm, comforting, drawing her into caring, secure arms that wouldn't let her fall when she was at her most helpless. It took a moment for her to notice the quiet breathing beside her bed, it seemed so ambient, so in line with the peaceful thoughts drifting through her mind. When she finally realised it her eyes popped open again, involuntarily, and wide with fear.

A beautiful woman stood next to her bed, staring down at Odette with a strange expression in her bright blue almond-shaped eyes. She was dressed completely in black; black leather gloves, a black corset, black leather leggings, black steel-toed boots, and an open black trench-coat. Her long scarlet hair cascaded in curls around her shoulders, framing her fair diamond-shaped face. She was short, barely taller than Odette herself, but she carried herself with a demeanour that radiated confidence and competence. Odette noticed all these things in a fraction of a second, but what really drew her attention was the old-fashioned flintlock pistol shoved through her belt and the silver-handled knife in her left hand. Both weapons were ornate; the pistol had a dark brown wooden handle, engraved on each side with the red image of a fire-breathing dragon, and the knife had a short, keenly sharp leaf-shaped blade, with a hilt engraved with pictures of a tree and a horse's head. Odette opened her mouth to scream, but the woman clamped her right hand firmly over her lips before a single sound could trickle forth. Odette's eyes grew even wider now, the woman had moved with incredible speed.

"This isn't the place for introductions," the woman whispered, in a soft comforting voice that belied the hard look in her eyes. Without another word she pulled Odette from her bed, and steadied her standing on the floor.

"Don't make a sound," she cautioned, looking firmly into Odette's eyes. Still cradling the knife in a deceptively relaxed manner in her left palm, she grabbed ahold of Odette's hand with a steel grip and pulled her towards the door.

"Come along," she hissed. "Don't make me drag you." They exited Odette's door and headed down the stairs. The strange woman's footfalls didn't make a sound, and Odette wondered how she could be so silent in such heavy boots. They cut through the darkened kitchen and out the back door. It was freezing cold outside, and Odette was only wearing a night-gown. The frigid air cut through her skin as if it weren't there, chilling her bones and her blood. She was shivering within a minute of the woman pulling her forcefully down the slick wet street.

"I . . . I'm g-going to freeze to d-death," she forced out through rattling teeth, wrapping her free arm around her trembling body. A small red car flashed past them, illuminating them for a moment in soft yellow light, before it disappeared around a corner, leaving them behind in the harsh cold. The woman stopped and turned around, releasing Odette's hand for the first time. For a fraction of a second the idea of running away flashed across Odette's mind but she swiftly dismissed that foolishness. The woman shrugged off her trench-coat and draped it around Odette's thin shaking shoulders. The girl hugged it around herself gratefully, slipping her hands inside the long sleeves. The woman was left with nothing covering her own shoulders or her well-muscled arms, but she didn't seem to even feel the cold.

"Come along, Odette," she said in her deceptively soft, sweet voice. She set off down the road, allowing Odette to follow her of her own free will.

"How do you know my name?" Odette asked, feeling a little bolstered by this show of trust and by the woman's kindness.

"It's my business," the woman replied without looking back.

"Where are we going?" Odette pressed.

"That is also my business," came the soft reply. There was no menace in her words or her tone, but somehow Odette felt a quiet chill in her soul. She didn't ask any more questions. They headed east; the mysterious woman walking at a pace so fast that Odette had to half-run to keep up with her. At the first intersection they reached, the woman turned north. There was very little traffic, but the woman stuck to the side of the road and Odette stayed directly behind her. After about fifteen minutes of walking, the woman turned down a dark alley, composed of packed frozen mud. About halfway down the alley she stopped at a tall iron fence. A savage-looking grey dog with a spiked collar came rushing through the darkness, crashing into the bars, barking and growling ferociously. The woman ignored it, staring off into the sky for a long moment. A few stars could be seen twinkling, but Odette couldn't be sure what she was looking at. Finally she looked down at the frothing guard dog.

"Silence," she commanded in an authoritative tone. The dog's barking immediately ceased and he just sat and stared at the woman, an almost quizzical look in his chocolate brown eyes. She produced a large silver key from a small pouch on her belt and inserted it into the lock on the fence's gate. It swung open, creaking, and she strode through into the muddy yard. Odette followed her timidly, fearfully eyeing the dog, but it continued to stare at the woman in silence. The woman walked decisively to a small shed sitting in the yard. Discarding the silver key back into the pouch, she produced a small golden one, which she inserted into the shed door's padlock and turned with a click. She turned and looked at Odette, an unreadable expression in her bright eyes. "After you, mademoiselle," she said, pushing the shed door open.

Odette saw a spider-web strung across the top of the door frame, but she swallowed down her fear and stepped into the pitch black of the shed. The woman followed close behind her, swinging the shed door shut. As soon as the latch clicked, Odette heard the guard dog explode into another frenzy of barking, directed at the shed. The woman struck a match, lighting a cob-webbed wax candle that sat in a holder on the wall. It filled the shed with a buttery golden light, and Odette looked around in curiosity. The walls were painted dark purple, a colour which struck her as strange for a shed. Several cardboard boxes full of the bodies of decapitated dolls sat in the middle of the floor. The heads rolled around in sawdust around Odette's feet, all of them missing their eyes. Old spider-webs festooned every corner of the shed. A beautiful red butterfly fluttered frantically in one of them, fruitlessly attempting to extricate itself from its sticky peril. A large bronze statue of Buddha with a dead rat lodged in its mouth stood against the far wall, solemnly staring across the shed. Blood trickled down his solemn chubby jaw.

"What is this place?" Odette whispered, as the woman walked over to the Buddha, grabbed it by the head and threw it down on the ground. She picked up a medieval-looking double-bladed axe that had been leaning up against the wall behind it. She took a step back, surveying the wall that the Buddha had been standing against. Then she suddenly swung the axe back and buried it deep in the purple wood. It splintered and cracked under the powerful blow. She struck at the wall again and again, until she had demolished a hole as tall as she was in it, then tossed the axe aside. It clattered and rang against the ground as it bounced around. Odette stepped forward cautiously, peering around the woman at what she had been cutting towards. It looked like a dripping wall of mud, with some strange designs in it. It took Odette a moment to realise they were screaming mask-like faces, oddly distorted and twisted. She shuddered and looked away.

"Take my hand," the woman instructed, holding out her black-gloved fingers. Odette slipped her pale slender hand into them obediently. The woman immediately stepped into the gruesome mudslide. Odette dug her feet into the ground to avoid being pulled in after, but she was helpless against the mysterious stranger's steel strength. She felt the mud striking the top of her head for only a split second before she stumbled through it. The woman released her hand and she staggered and fell down. The ground was soft and wet, grass blades dancing delicately in a gentle wind. A vast number of stars shone in the night sky, there was no trace of the fog that had just swirled around them on the street. Odette rolled over onto her back to look up, and saw a great number of tall trees surrounding her, reaching up to the full moon. The strange woman stood motionless, like a stone statue, in the middle of the meadow they were in, staring off into the darkness. Odette rolled over again, onto her elbows, trying to follow the woman's gaze, but she saw nothing but some swaying bushes and then black beyond it. She slowly stood to her feet, turning in a slow circle to take in her environment.

They were in a thin forest, oak and ash and elm; despite the darkness, it didn't feel menacing at all, it actually felt quite safe, especially after the horrific shed. Suddenly the strange woman began to whistle, softly at first, but steadily growing louder, a strange whimsical tune that awakened strange emotions in Odette's heart. The girl turned to look at her kidnapper, and was shocked by the utterly blank look in her eyes. She stood utterly inert, save for her full scarlet lips, which were pursed in the creation of the peculiar whistling. Odette strained her ears, but the only other sound she could hear was the faint breeze rustling the leaves of the trees. Then she heard a strange voice, somewhere in the far-off distance, singing in tune with the woman's whistling. The words were faint, but she could make them out.

Watching as my red blood drips,
White birds scatter as I touch my lips,
Floating away on their worldly trips,
Leaving nothing but water,
Touching my hand to a withering tree,
When will I open my eyes to see,
All the creatures staring at me,
I am nobody's daughter . . .

Both the singing and the whistling faded away as a strange, but somehow familiar, creature emerged from the dark bushes. It had the body of a man, dressed rather sharply in a black tuxedo with a frilled white shirt and a navy blue tie. But Odette barely even noticed that, she was staring aghast at the thing's head. It was the head of a stuffed horse, its brown coat ragged and thread-worn, patched with bits of white and pink stripes, red plaid, and dark blue. It had a white mane and black glass eyes marred by deep scratches. The woman snapped out of her trance as he approached, and smiled at him.

"I've got her," she said, briefly indicating the shocked Odette, who was still staring with mouth slightly ajar.

"Excellent," the bizarre creature replied in a clear, cultured voice, treating Odette to the most summary of glances before returning his attention to the woman. His mouth didn't move when he spoke. "We have many things to discuss," he was addressing the woman. "Nicholas has obtained some important information about the Metropolitan airship routes. Meanwhile . . ." Odette heard an odd tapping sound. A moment later the horse-headed man was standing behind her, and she felt a prick in her shoulder.

The only thing Odette felt at first when her eyes opened was the ache in the muscles of her right arm. Slowly, however, other information filtered in. She was lying on a bed of soft springy moss inside a dirty beige canvas tent. She could hear the sound of a large fire crackling outside the tent and low voices talking. She couldn't hear the words, but she recognised the tones of the horse-headed man and the mysterious woman who had kidnapped her. She lay still, wondering what the best course of action was. She didn't feel like escape was a viable option with that woman around. Not to mention she wouldn't have the vaguest idea where to escape to, she didn't even know where she was being held hostage. She was in some forest out in the country, obviously nowhere near when they had walked through that strange portal in the shed. It took her a moment to realise it when the voices outside stopped, she had been lost in her own thoughts. She held her breath, straining to hear even the slightest sound outside the tent. She jumped in fright, gasping frantically, when the bizarre creature from the woods suddenly pushed aside the tent flap and walked inside the tent. Once again she was struck by how weirdly familiar he seemed.

"Sorry if I startled you," he said in an apologetic tone, pushing his fingers into a steeple. "Also my sincere condolences for the shot, we simply had to transport you quickly and that was the safest way."

"Where am I?" Odette asked, sitting up. This creature, as strange as it was, seemed harmless enough.

"Deep in the Yellow Forest," he said. "But where are my manners . . . are you hungry?"

"Yeah," Odette admitted, a little sheepishly as her stomach gurgled. She had forgotten about food in all the heady rush of excitement.

"Come with me," the creature said, gesturing for her to follow him. He exited the tent, and Odette followed suit. The scene she walked out onto was not much different from the one that had first greeted her on this side of the muddy portal. A wide clearing, surrounded by a thick ring of tall dark trees. There was a large bonfire burning near the tent, which was where the horse-headed man was walking. There was no sign of the woman anywhere.

"Who is she?" Odette asked, as she trailed behind the creature.

"Amelia?" he replied. "She is quite extraordinary, isn't she? I'll attempt to explain this, in a moment, don't fret. But first, lets get a little food in your stomach, you must be absolutely famished after your little trip." He produced a tin plate containing fried eggs, a green salad, and a chopped apple with tomato sauce poured over it. A knife and a fork lay crossed over it. Odette accepted it gratefully, despite the somewhat strange fare.

"Allow me to introduce myself," the horse-headed man said cordially. "My name is Rabbit."

Odette jumped again, staring at the creature with wide-eyed shock. He stared back, and she imagined if his eyes were capable of showing emotion they would have been quizzical. "Rabbit?" she finally repeated, somewhat stupidly.

"Indeed, Mademoiselle," he replied, steepling his fingers again.

"Oh my god," Odette sat down heavily on the ground, cradling her plate in her lap. "Oh my god."

"Is something the matter?" Rabbit tilted his head to the side, as if pondering something.

"No . . ." Odette said. "Its just . . . don't you remember me?"

"Should I?" Rabbit replied blankly.

"You were my stuffed horse . . . when I was six my parents got me it for my birthday and I had really wanted a rabbit so that's what I named you . . . I lost you when I was twelve, my foster parent's dog tore you up . . ." Odette's voice trailed off and she stared down at the food in her lap.

"Interesting," was the horse-headed man's only answer. He sat down cross-legged a few metres from Odette, turning to face her. "To be honest your eyes are far too sane to be the little lunatic many in the Forest Council are already painting you to be."

"Pardon?" said Odette.

"Our spies are excellent at gathering information," Rabbit continued. "We've seen you in the GMK, we've heard the whispers that Alexander has found some little puppet of a human girl to play goddess for him. Sacrilege in our eyes, many of the commanders were outraged. Several of them voted for Amelia to just kill you outright, but the cooler heads won through, quite fortunately for you."

"OK . . ." Odette said slowly, trying to focus on the one thing she somewhat understood. "Who is Amelia?"

"Archmurderer of the Trifektum," Rabbit replied. "She's a legend in the darkness. Simply put, she's the best assassin in the world, but she's also a great thief and spy, and a great commander. Half-human and half-darkfeeder."

"Trifektum?" Odette felt incapable of doing anything but numb questioning.

"An alliance of blood children. Humans, otherkin, spider clan, darkfeeders. We mostly live in the Yellow Forest, it's good cover from Metropolitan attacks and allows to operate as a guerrilla force. They had heavy advantage over us in numbers and technology until the Pestilence came. Now most of their cursed race lies sick in their precious hospital, but its been turned into an impenetrable fortress while they work on their cure. We do our best to interrupt their oil supplies, but any direct assault on the GMK would be a devastating loss for us. Eat, eat," he suddenly cried, noticing the food sitting untouched in Odette's lap.

"Why do you hate them . . . the Metropolitans?" She asked, obediently digging her utensils into the meal.

"They're cursed," Rabbit said. "And, besides that, they've always looked down on every other race, treated them like slaves. They consider us animals compared to them. Worst of all they have taken our faith, our deep belief in our ancient goddess, Odette, and warped it with their twisted souls and their tainted stolen artefact."

"The Tapestry?"

"Yes," Rabbit affirmed. "They stole it from the Temple of Blood some two hundred years ago, right before they burned it to the ground. That was when Alexander started going by the title 'High Priest'. He was just a regular Black Coat Commandant before that."

"Alexander is two hundred years old?" Odette was surprised at how good the tomato sauce tasted on apples.

"Almost three hundred," Rabbit said. "We don't know what's been keeping him alive so long. Metropolitans have long life-spans, but he's almost doubled the length of a ripe Metropolitan life now."

"Where are you going to take me?" Odette asked. She was convinced this was real, it didn't feel like a dream at all.

"To see the Forest Council," Rabbit replied. "Some of them will clamour for your head, but that's just to be expected. Amelia seems to think it's a good idea to keep you alive now, and she has a lot of influence. She seemed to have taken rather a shine to you, actually."

"Where did she go to?"

"Refuge. Its our secret headquarters in the Yellow Forest, where the Council stays. Well it use to be a closely-guarded secret, but we don't even worry about the Metros finding it anymore. They don't have the offensive power to come after us even if they did. We'll leave for there tomorrow, it will be a three or four day journey, depending on what kind of pace you can maintain."

"It will probably be four," Odette said wryly. Rabbit laughed, and Odette found it creepy, simply because his face and eyes never moved. She decided that saying something about it would probably hurt his feelings, and let that question go.

"We had better turn in soon," the horse-headed man said. "We'll need to get an early start tomorrow."

Odette stood before the Tapestry, in the little shrine that was growing so familiar. She gazed at it with an eager smile, but something was very wrong. The Tapestry sat unmoving, a frozen block of a single colour; blood red. She approached it, reaching out a finger to touch the wall. It felt like ice.

"Alexander!" she yelled, but the only response was the eerie echo of her own voice. She took a few steps backwards, looking the Tapestry up and down. Something wet fell on her face, and her hand flew to it, brushing it away. Then she heard the plop of something liquid splashing in the mud beside her. Another drop struck her, this time in her hair. She looked up at the vaulted ceiling of the room, which was strangely illuminated. It was covered in grotesque smeared blood. More and more drops of it trickled down, splashing their scarlet stains on her night-gown, on her skin, in her hair.

"Alexander!" she shouted again, desperately, but still there was no sign of her High Priest. The blood was falling like rain now, drenching her in its warm stickiness. Shading her eyes, she looked up at the ceiling again. Then she saw them, dozens of human corpses impaled on steel stalactites, scattered all over the ceiling, gaping black sockets where their eyes should be. Their blood was pouring down now in torrents, masses of crimson teardrops free-falling together into the mud.

"Alexander!" she was screaming now, fruitlessly trying to shield herself from the downpour with her hands. She turned her gaze back to the dead Tapestry, which stubbornly refused to move again no matter how hard she wished it. Her white night-gown was soaked red now, and scarlet droplets trickled across her pale skin like sweat. She felt a sick feeling rise in her churning stomach, and moments later she was on her knees, vomiting in the mud. She looked down at the green vile mess, tears streaming down her face. Where was everybody?

CHAPTER 10

kein hoffnung für die tinte

"I'm so scared of the dark that I'm afraid to close my eyes."

Odette woke up sitting bolt upright in her bed. She stared around her room, shock settling into her system. Where was Rabbit, and the great forest of tall dark trees? She scrambled out of her bed, falling onto her knees and rubbing the carpet beneath her with her palms, picking at the strands with her fingers. She wasn't sure if this was real, or if it was another dream like the Tapestry . . . She crawled over to the wall of her room, running her hands along its cold surface. It felt real, but so had the food Rabbit had fed her last night. The roaring bonfire, the cool night breeze . . . But this, this felt more familiar. Her carpet, her wall, her bed. She sat on her knees, looking around the plain little room, trying to filter out the distortions of reality. Everything felt hazy, cocooned in a wet clinging fog. She whirled around as a shadow dashed swiftly across the corner of her eye, but all she saw was more of her room.

"Who's there?" she whispered, wavering back and forth on the carpet. Her whole room was bathed in cold grey light, little suspicious shadows dancing in the corners. A level, emotionless voice started speaking in the back of her mind, enunciating each word with calculated precision.

Running towards our third demise,
Blackened hearts and blackened souls,
No one watching our blood rise,
These highways all have deadly tolls,
But we travel on them nonetheless,
Recalling the cures we swallowed down,
Searching for a god to bless,
Punishing a tarnished crown,
These things that ferment in my mind,
This pain I know so very well,
Sometimes I wonder if God is blind,
Is he watching when I'm in hell.

"Who was that?" Odette's voice sounded thin in the tiny room, barely piercing the long cold silence that followed the solemnly delivered words. She whirled around again, but there was nothing but familiarity all around, overcast by menacing shadows. Nothing moved except her body, which heaved up and down with rapid breathing. Calm. Her eyes moved suspiciously across the walls and the floor, examining and re-examining every aspect of this room that she simply should not be in. Breathe. It took a lot of concentration, she felt on the verge of panic. The beleaguered walls of her reality felt as if they were finally crashing down, all around her cowering form. But raised arms could do nothing to shield her from an avalanche of living stone.

Odette shrieked aloud as a vibrant knock shook her door slightly, echoing through her mind. It was swiftly followed by Marie's worried sounding voice. "Are you alright, sweetie?" Odette ran her hands through her hair, her lips trembling but suddenly stricken, unable to produce coherent sound, wilfully disobeying their mistress' orders. The door creaked as Marie turned the doorknob, slowly pushing it open. She peeked her head around the edge of it, her face filled with concern. Odette looked up at her with incomprehension in her blue eyes, numbness spreading across the skin of her face. Her lips still quivering, but all that issued forth was a quiet whimpering sound, so soft that Marie wasn't sure she heard it. She stepped towards the cowering girl slowly, keeping her tone low and sweet.

"What's wrong, sweetie?" she asked, looking down into Odette's disoriented face. Marie knelt down on the floor, reaching out a hand to touch Odette's shoulder. The girl looked down at it numbly as their skin met. She could feel it, but something in her mind was chaotically screaming that none of this was real. And if this wasn't real, what was? Maybe everything was a dream and she just couldn't wake up.

"Odette?" Marie asked in a soft voice as the girl's wandered away from her and started roving around the room.

"Where am I?" Odette finally forced her lips to articulate the question that was consuming her mind. She kept looking around the room, waiting for something to change, for it all to shimmer away and leave her stranded in some other strange reality, lost in the darkness.

"You're here . . . in our house, in your room," Marie answered, deftly hiding her own confusion. "Safe."

"Safe?" Odette repeated it almost automatically. It didn't seem like a very likely possibility, being safe, but it wasn't something she had thought about.

"Yes, safe, sweetie," Marie's confirmation was laden with quiet authority, but Odette still wasn't entirely convinced. Too many shadows dancing, who could watch them all . . .

"Puppets," Odette whispered, closing her eyes. Too many of them to watch, it was hurting her eyes. They ran about as if no laws restrained them at all, cast by a renegade fantasy.

"Do you want to come down and eat breakfast?" Marie asked quietly, gently rubbing Odette's shoulder.

"What if its not for my real stomach?" Odette moaned, clasping her hands over her eyelids. Breathe.

"It is, sweetie, its real food," Marie assured her. She took Odette's wrists, pulling her hands down from her eyes. "Open your eyelids up, darling," she said. "It's OK."

For a moment they remained frozen in place, but then Odette's eyelids fluttered spasmodically before finally springing open. Marie smiled, and offered her hand to the girl, who took it slowly, staring blankly ahead of her. "Come on," Marie said, pulling Odette up to her feet. "Lets go eat."

The Schillers and Odette sat around the small kitchen table, a breakfast of brötchen and omelettes on their plates.

Odette picked at her food aimlessly, painfully aware of both of them staring at her over the tops of their coffee mugs. The look in Marie's eyes was one of concern and worry, the look in Dieter's was . . . different. Breathe. She forced herself to swallow down a sizeable hunk of brötchen, chasing it with a dash of steaming coffee. She wanted to just close her eyes, let the darkness consume her and shield her, but she resisted the urge. Eat, keep up your strength, blah blah. She forced herself to swallow down another bite, not wishing to be on the receiving end of that speech. They thought she was fucked up enough as it was, without throwing an eating disorder on top of the pile. She tried not to look at Dieter, every time she saw that predatory gleam in his eyes she almost spiralled into panic. Breathe. Fuck.

"Do you have anything going on today, Odette?" Marie asked, breaking the crystalline silence. The prismatic pieces glimmered a rainbow of colours as they shattered on the hard floor.

"I have, um, football practice tonight," Odette mumbled, before pushing another forkful across her lips. She stared down at her plate, she couldn't bear looking into any of the eyes fixed so intently on her. She felt like they were going to swallow her up. Others started to light up in the darkness, blinking once a minute as they studiously followed her every movement. Keen and piercing, attached to unknown entities. Odette wanted to scream at them, but she knew there would just be a frozen silence in return. And the Schillers were still there, reigning over the rest. They already thought she was crazy, there was no point in heaping more fuel on the fire she was chained inside.

"Good," Odette could feel, rather than see, Marie smiling, as she finally replied. "That's fun." Odette just inclined her head slightly, a neutral expression on her face. She wasn't in the mood to act enthused. She still wasn't convinced that this was all real, but she wasn't prepared to test her suspicions with anything dramatic. She might be wrong, after all. *The answer to all our questions lies in our graves.* She tried not to look surprised in front of the Schillers, but it wasn't her voice that echoed in the back of her mind. It was a strange one, sepulchral and melancholy, that echoed strangely, as if playing against stones. *It's better for business, dear.* Odette clamped her hands to the sides of her head, trying vainly to drive the voice away.

"Is everything OK, Odette?" she heard Marie's voice in the distance somewhere, muffled by walls and locked doors. She would have to scream if she wanted a reply. Odette looked around in the darkness; water trickled down grey stone walls, splashing on the ground, and chains rattled against iron bars as they were drawn slowly across them. Something bearing a glittering sword and a flickering torch stalked by in the darkness, it's face obscured by a chain-mesh mask.

"Odette?" The vision shimmered and faded as Marie's voice cut through it again, replete with the strains of worry.

"Yeah, I'm OK," Odette answered hastily, taking a bite of omelette in an attempt to fortify her self-diagnosis. She sneaked a glance up at Marie, but the woman's brooding eyes didn't look convinced. *Breathe.* Odette stabbed angrily at the remains of her breakfast, desperately wishing she could escape from this prison of staring eyes.

It encircled her imperiously, embedding barbed wires run through blood-soaked chains in her skin. They tightened and tightened, forcing a thick ooze to bubble out of her veins, squeezing out onto the floor. She felt light-headed, sweat pounding across her brow, veins burning up with protest at their tortured state. Her hand gripped the edge of the table so hard that her knuckles turned white, before it slipped away, too slick to maintain its grasp. It fell limp into her lap, twitching spasmodically as if it were being poked with a stick by a curious child. She knew the Schillers must be staring at her by now, but they said nothing, or at least she couldn't hear them. Breathe. Why the fuck couldn't she breathe?

Odette could still feel the scars burning lividly on her arm as she walked silently beside Anna towards school. She had managed to escape from the clutches of the Schiller's house, dodging Marie's worried questions about whether she was alright to go to school. Of course she wasn't alright, but she went every day when she wasn't alright, didn't she? Anna was uncharacteristically quiet, she sensed Odette's inner turmoil and knew when it was simply best to be silent. Odette would talk when she was ready. She kept massaging her own arm, because even though there were no visible marks she could still feel the trail of the barbed wire's agonising punctures. She couldn't stop herself from constantly glancing down, as if evidence of the pain would suddenly emerge.

"Why did you run away from me?" Suddenly Rabbit was walking on her left side, his immobile face staring straight ahead.

"I didn't," Odette hissed. Anna glanced at her briefly, but she knew she wasn't being addressed.

"I trusted you," Rabbit continued. "I could have tied you up . . . the Trifektum would have liked that. I could have knocked you out, hurt you . . . you were a prisoner of war, I could have treated you however I saw fit. Most of the Council derides you as a puppet of Alexander's. But I didn't, I treated you with the kindness and respect that I think everyone, even the cursed Metropolitans and their mindless slaves, deserves. And yet I fall asleep and when I awake my sparrow is flown. Curses on my head for being such a fool. The Council will surely agree."

"I didn't run on purpose," the pain in Odette's shoulder flared up suddenly, and she gritted her teeth. "I just . . . I just woke up and I was back home."

"Home? And where do you call home, little marionette?" Even though his sewn face remained unmoving as always, Odette could hear the unmasked disgust in Rabbit's voice. "The cursed hospital of your master? Alexander erected those white palisades as a tomb for his own race, and it will be your tomb too if you don't break free of his control. They're all doomed, every oil-sipping son of a bitch cowering in that sterilised safety."

Odette stopped walking and turned slowly towards the Trifektum agent, a strange curiosity sparkling in her eyes. He stopped as well, but his face and eerie glass pupils remained fixed forward. "And where are we now?"

"Wherever you want to be," Rabbit answered after a long moment, before shimmering and fading away.

"Odette?" Anna was walking backwards about five metres down the road, holding her books to her stomach. "You OK?"

"Yeah," Odette spoke slowly, chewing over each syllable, still staring at the empty space left by Rabbit's sudden disappearance. "Yeah. I'm coming. Wait up."

"Odette, what the fuck is going on?" Anna demanded, as Odette drew even with her again. "You've been acting so strange the last couple of days."

"I've just been seeing a lot of weird stuff," Odette tried to sound airy. "It's been hard to focus."

Anna had hardly believed her, but she had at least let the subject drop for the rest of the day.

"One touch!" Mrs. Biewer shouted, presiding over the rows of girls passing footballs back and forth. Odette was having difficulty dispelling the swirling thoughts that plagued her, even with all the mindless drills to help.

"Two touches!"

Hilde, Odette's passing partner, stopped the ball in front of her and sent it skidding back across the grass. Odette responded to the action mindlessly, her eyes fixed on the rotating white orb.

Traps, shots, running, none of it helped.

"Are you OK?" Hilde sat down on the wooden bench next to Odette, picking up a glass bottle of mineral water. "You seem a little out of it."

Odette just shrugged, unsure of what to say. Hilde went to the same school as she did, but they never talked outside of football. "Not really," she finally answered. She was tired of lying about it.

"What's wrong?" Hilde asked, taking a swig from the bottle.

Odette just shrugged again. She didn't know how to say it in a way that didn't sound insane. Everything was so fucked.

"You're friends with that Anna girl, right?"

"Yeah," Odette answered, surprised.

"She's a little frightening," Hilde smiled.

"She's alright," Odette answered. She felt that her tone should have been more defensive than it was. Anna was Anna, after all.

Tempo! Tempo!

The door shutting behind Odette sounded hollow, like a metal pipe clanging down a shaft. Dieter was perched in his arm chair watching some cop show on the TV. Odette took a few trembling steps towards the stairs, freezing in place when he turned his head to look at her.

"How was your day?" he asked, in a perfectly normal conversational tone. The room felt like it was shrinking from the corners, strange drumming sounds thundering in Odette's ears. It was all she could do to keep from collapsing to the floor in a pile of cold sweat and clammy skin.

"Fine," she finally forced out. Everything felt so surreal, he looked so likeable . . . "Is Marie here?" What if I'm imagining all of this?

"She went out to shop," he answered, in a voice that triggered a new jolt of fear shooting down Odette's spine. She stood and stared into the man's eyes for a long moment, trying to read the thoughts behind his innocent blue expression. The air felt thick around her, compressing, oppressing. Suddenly she turned on her heels and ran up the stairs with the desperation of a trapped rat, scrabbling helplessly against a crushing wall. She heard Dieter's heavy, measured footsteps behind her, and she could have sworn she heard him laughing. In a brief moment of clarity she dashed into the bathroom, slamming the door behind her and fumbling frantically with the lock. It clicked in place just as his hand turned the doorknob.

"Odette," his voice was soothing, calming. "What's wrong?"

"Stay away from me!" she screamed, cowering down against the wall.

"Don't be silly, Odette," he answered, thumping his hand forcefully against the wood. "If one of your hallucinations is scaring you, you should talk to somebody. Are you OK?" One of my hallucinations.

"Just go away!"

"Odette, just open the door. I can't let you hurt yourself in there. I'm going to have to call Stefani if you don't come out."

I didn't make it up, I couldn't have. It wasn't a hallucination. At the mention of Stefani's name her voice rang in Odette's head, instructing her about the symptoms of schizophrenia.

"You won't always know."

"Odette, please don't hurt yourself," Dieter's voice carried a note of concern that reminded her of Marie.

"I'm not. Go away!" she yelled, burying her head in her arms. Tears came flowing unbidden from her eyes, running onto the tiny frightened hairs on her arm. I can't be wrong. I'm not wrong. Please say I'm not wrong.

"Odette, you don't have to come out, just please unlock the door. You could be killing yourself for all I know. What's going on?"

"Please stop. Just stop, please." Her confidence felt shaken, water rushing across her memories; distorted, vague, a shimmer of uncertainty. Was none of it real? I'm sick. I'm really, really sick. I'm going to destroy everything if I don't control it. Fuck, fuck, fuck.

"Odette, I'm going to have to take the door off if you don't unlock it."

"Wait," she called out. Her nails dragged painfully across the tiles as she staggered to her feet. It didn't make sense, she had to be wrong; please, please, God, let me be wrong. Marie and Dieter love me, they care about me . . . the lock clicked twice in the doorknob, and the door swung open fast, far too fast. Dieter grabbed her with crushing force, the only love in it so twisted and mangled as to be unrecognisable. She fought back for only a moment before she was fully overpowered by the adult man. She was pushed screaming and crying against the wall, torn and battered. Please, God.

CHAPTER 11

angst

The first sensation Odette felt was a loud whirring noise all around her. She was standing in a long narrow hallway of stark brown metal. Steam hissed from between the cracks of sealed doors and from rapidly rotating spouts in the ceiling. The floor echoed hollowly beneath her feet as she took several timid steps forward, peering around her for any signs of life. Everything here seemed mechanised, dead, an uncaring clockwork organism. There was a large metal door with a wheel at the end of the hall. It was cracked open slightly, filtering through a sliver of musty grey light. Odette made her way towards it slowly, constantly looking to the left and right, half-expecting strange monsters to leap out of the walls. The whirring sounds grew in volume as she drew closer to the door, until she could no longer hear herself breathe. She peeked through the crack in the door, but all she could see was a fairly bleak brown room. She could just make out the tip of what resembled some form of control console, but she couldn't hear or see anybody. She had to shove the door several times to get it to open wide enough for her to slip inside; it was extremely heavy. There was a Metropolitan wearing a brown pilot's jacket and flight goggles sitting in front of the console, busily adjusting knobs and control levers. When she heard the door creak she whirled around, pulling a revolver from a holster on her leather belt.

"Who are you?" she snapped, her voice clipped and business-like. "How did you get on this ship? Are you a Trifektum terrorist? Let me see your hands, slowly."

Odette looked around the room, largely ignoring the Metropolitan's orders. It looked kind of like a cockpit, but much larger. The walls were metal, the floor was metal, and it was all covered with gears and knobs and turning dials.

"Where am I?" Odette asked hazily, her brain slowly trying to process everything around her. None of this seemed right.

The pilot's gun faltered slightly, and lowered for a moment, but then she brought it up again quickly. "Who are you?" she repeated. "Don't move!" as Odette started to venture over to the control panel to look at it more closely.

"Who are you?"

"Uh . . ." Odette's mind felt frozen, sluggish. "I'm not really sure."

The Metropolitan cocked the revolver, levelling it even with Odette's chest. "Don't fuck around with me, kid," she snapped. "Are you suppose to sabotage this mission? Are the explosives already planted?" Suddenly, she pointed the gun at the floor, turning her back on Odette.

The Tapestry of Odette

"Ah, it's probably a suicide anyway." She sat down heavily in her chair, putting her feet up on the console.

"So how much longer do we have?"

"I didn't put any bombs on this . . . whatever this is," Odette shrugged. "I don't even know how I got here. I was just standing there in the hall, and I can't remember what was happening before. I . . . I think it was bad though. I'm not sure." What the fuck . . .

The Metropolitan spun around in her chair to face Odette. Her harsh bird-like eyes surveyed her from head to toe, coldly, calculating. It reminded her of Alexander's hooded stare, the eyes hiding more than they revealed.

What is water? In a dream world covered by falling leaves and the subtle suggestion of genocide.

"How can you not know . . ." Odette's mouth began to speak, before her brain could cut it off.

"My name is Lucy," the Metropolitan said, ignoring whatever Odette had started to say. Maybe she hadn't said it at all. "I'm the pilot and commander of this airship, Herrschaft *über* Abschaum."

Dreaming.

"Where are we going?" Odette asked, turning to look out the large windows at the front of the cockpit. A vast green forest lay before them, conifers and oaks spreading out as far as the eye could see.

"The Bad Ölfeld. It's in Trifektum territory, but it used to be the largest supplier of oil to the GMK. There are untapped riches there that our High Priest is eager to utilise." All of it seemed like it should make sense, but none of it did. Odette's head hurt.

"Can I have some water?" Her throat ached from dryness.

Lucy cocked her head to the side quizzically. "What is water?" She asked, eyes betraying true ignorance.

"Um . . . never mind," Odette wandered over to the windows, wondering how you couldn't know what water is. Even when she tried to redirect her thoughts to other areas, it nagged at the back of her brain, strange and inexplicable.

Dreaming.

"We'll be at the oil fields in about half an hour," Lucy stated in a matter-of-fact fashion. She seemed to be accepting Odette appearing out of nothing altogether too readily. Maybe that sort of thing was normal here. Wherever here was. It all seemed intoxicatingly familiar, but Odette couldn't remember why. She couldn't remember what she expected normalcy to be like either, so maybe this was it. But it all seemed too strange to be something she had grown up with. Of course, that could be the trick of it. Tricky little bastard. Fucking gypsy. Odette wrinkled her brow, unsure how to handle the random thoughts that shot through her mind. It was difficult enough for her to control which ones she chose to voice, let alone sort them into anything that made even a remnant of logical sense.

I touched a flower yesterday,
It withered and curled away from my hand,
Its scarlet hues faded to grey,
I cried that I didn't understand,
I dipped my finger into a watery pool,
It darkened in righteous anger at me,
It asked how could I be so cruel,
To torment it for eternity,

I wandered into a beautiful meadow,
The green grass died around my feet,
I wept to my heartless shadow,
The rain around me turned to sleet,
I fall to my knees screaming my sorrow,
Beauty dies before my sight,
Through the darkness I can't see tomorrow,
Snuffing out my only light . . .

The song faded away as the oil fields came into sight, vast deep pools of bubbling darkness, separated by thick, drenched black mud. The airship came to a vertical resting place on a small empty ridge on the edge of the fields.

Lucy picked her way through the bubbling black fields, followed closely by a carefully stepping Odette. The ground beneath them was soft sludge, it reminded Odette of the Tapestry chamber. Small rivulets of oil, festering and hissing like magma, crawled their way between the dark pools. Odette glanced over her shoulder at the idle airship, and was surprised to see dozens of small creatures scattering back and forth between the airship and the rich oil fields. They walked on a set of four robotic legs, which retracted to be replaced by emerging wheels when coasting over smooth ground. They had long, extendable arms with huge claws at the end, in which they carried the massive grey metal barrels that contained the Metropolitan lifeblood. They had no bodies to speak of, just a thin platform on which their arms and peculiar heads were mounted. These metallic heads were slender and tapered, with two huge glowing green eyes set in them. The heads swivelled back and forth, three hundred and sixty degrees, as if they were watching for something.

"What are those things?" Odette asked, slightly out of breath, as Lucy's swift shambling pace was difficult to keep up with.

"They're Ambrosian Walkers," Lucy replied with a hint of pride in her voice. "They're a sentient mechanical race from south of the Yellow Forest. We use them to harvest oil and other pedestrian tasks. We conquered them a hundred and forty years ago under the tutelage of the esteemed Alexander, and they have been our loyal servants since. Like us, they do not require blood, so they would never have been accepted into the zealous folds of the Trifektum."

"So where are we going now?" Odette pressed, narrowly avoiding plunging headlong into an oil pool.

"One of my favourite places," Lucy replied mysteriously. She seemed confident, and familiar with the terrain, so Odette pushed aside further questioning and attempted to follow the Metropolitan's footsteps more closely.

Soon they came to a small hill, on top of which was perched a single desolate tree, towering gigantic above them. It was leafless, blackened by soot and fumes, long dead but still standing. Lucy climbed up the hill and sat down beneath it, looking up at the clouded sky through the empty branches. Odette followed her, but stood a distance from the tree, looking at it suspiciously. It looked familiar, but Odette wasn't sure why. Déjà vu. She stood silently staring at this lone survivor of an apocalypse, courageously persisting through the bleak, lifeless centuries, a twisted beacon of hope so broken and defeated that it resembled its conquerors more than its former self.

"Come here, child," a voice, strained, ancient, spoke from the tree's trunk. Odette took a few tentative steps forward, peering at the blackened trunk.

"Closer," the voice spoke again; it sounded like an old man on the verge of death. Odette glanced at Lucy, but she was just staring out over the oil fields, seemingly oblivious.

"Only the Children of Blood can hear my voice," the tree said, in response to Odette's quizzical look. "Darkness clouds her ears."

Why?

"The Metropolitans are the Children of Death and cold mechanisation. They can not hear the whispers of the trees and the grass, the voice of the fallen moon. The world is simply a resource to be harvested. I have stood here for three thousand years, resisting every effort to tear me down, to poison me, but even I can not persist much longer. Once I was the Lord and Master of every tree within the Yellow Forest, but I have long been cast down. But, in my demise, I will watch my eternal enemies fall."

How?

"When one such as I dies, a god of the forest, it is no small matter. From my roots many spores have stirred, angry, destructive, created in my twilight for my revenge. They have been carried forth by the wind to punish my enemies, and they will be the end of them before I finally fall."

You mean the Dark Blight comes from you?

"Is that what they are calling it? Yes, the disease that is decimating the Metropolitan race was produced here. If you can, bring news of this to the Trifektum. My old

107

friend, the Sapphire Werewolf, will be pleased to hear it. Be alert, child, you are not alone."

The tree's voice faded away, and even though Odette walked up to it and put her ear against the bark, she could not hear the slightest trace of it. She suddenly looked up, as a high-pitched whistling sound burst out from the ridge where the airship was. Lucy leapt athletically to her feet. "The walker distress signal," she hissed, pulling her revolver from her belt. "Raiders."

She went racing down the hill. Odette tried to follow her, but she couldn't even begin to keep up with the Metropolitan, who soon disappeared among the pools and columns of fume. A gun shot rang out ahead of her, then another.

"Lucy!" Odette screamed, trying to avoid falling into any of the oil pools. Suddenly the thick air was riddled with deafening sound, the sound of the airship taking off. Odette tried to move faster, but she could only proceed at an agonisingly slow pace.

When she finally arrived at the airship's location, the craft was gone. Dozens of Ambrosian corpses were scattered about, some shot, others severed into pieces by blades. Lucy's pearl-handled revolver lay in the mud. Odette picked it up gingerly with both hands. One shot had been fired from it, but there was no sign of blood anywhere, so she must have missed whoever her target was. Assuming they had blood, which was far from a guarantee in this place. All of the Ambrosians appeared to be completely destroyed, so questioning them as to what had happened was out of the question.

Searching for diamonds in the dark clouds of pain.

CHAPTER 12

was ist wasser?

är vad bevattnar?

Odette sat up, dozens of strange memories washing through her head, faster than she could control. The room around her spun and shook, white running into white. Her palms slapped into the carpet, trying to control the rush and flow of the world, slipping and falling into the gaping abyss. Something about spores flowed through her brain, but it was gone before she could catch it. Blood flowed from the roof in the corners of her eyes, but disappeared with every searching turn of her head. She finally realised that she was on the floor in her bedroom, but she was unsure of the time, and even of the day. She staggered to her feet. Her T-shirt was torn, and there were dark stains that looked like blood on it. What the fuck is going on?

She discarded the destroyed article of clothing, pulling a new shirt from her dresser drawer. It was very quiet in the house, she guessed that neither Dieter nor Marie were home. She looked up at the clock on her roof . . . it read seven hundred, she guessed Wednesday morning, but she couldn't be sure. Everything felt so strange and surreal. Searching for diamonds . . . why was she searching for diamonds? Or for water, she didn't understand that either. She cracked her door open, poking her head out into the hallway, but she couldn't see any sign of either of the Schillers. Blood-stained white feathers drifted down from the roof, covering the floor in a soft, tainted cushion. She stared at them for a long moment, stretching her hand out to touch them several times, but always pulling it back. They looked intensely familiar, lying there, tarnished and desecrated . . .

When her fingers finally touched them they melted into shimmering powder, disappearing through the floor. She scrambled around on her hands and knees, searching for the thousand tiny holes that had ferreted them away, but she found nothing but carpet and frustration. Screaming, she slammed her hand into the floor until it was numb, reddened and aching. She withdrew into a corner, a safe resting-place, nursing her damaged hand and whimpering. Nothing had ever made any logical sense, but even her comfortable feelings of surrealism were fading away, replaced with something that intensely frightened her, dark and unknown. The Tapestry was her gateway to everything she would never understand, but still she was drawn to it, hypnotic, melodic, soothing songs of darkness surrounding. She felt an overwhelming urge to scream and break things, break everything, to fucking destroy the world, but she stayed cowering in her corner. Darkness swirled around the room, streaked with bruised purple, the ashes of burning feathers condemned to hell.

Better for business.

Odette stood in the bathroom with the door close, studying her reflection in the mirror. Her date with Bastian was tonight, a fact that had never completely escaped her mind. She glanced at the flat light-pad, then back to the mirror, twirling the tips of her hair in her fingers. Anna would laugh so hard at her right now, either that or spit. The strangeness that had been haunting her since morning had not fully disappeared, it had been in the back of her mind throughout the torturous school day. Always disappearing around the corner, but the whistling never fell out of ear-shot. Remember to wet your whistle!

Odette shook her head, looking down into the basin of the sink. She had to concentrate, she couldn't fall apart at the seams. She looked back into the mirror, but it had disappeared. The Tapestry stood in its place, a chaotic whirl of pink and brown and orange. The colours didn't fade into the floor as they usually did but were continuously swirled into a vortex in the middle, mixing together into the deepest black. New shades of colour were constantly injected into the rapidly rotating circle, fed into the ravenous whirlpool. Odette stared numbly at the centre of the Tapestry, leaning closer and closer towards it until her eyes were only centimetres from the black hole. She saw nothing, an endless continuation of nothing, all-devouring, all-destroying, all-consuming.

It took everything, every sacred colour, from her beloved Tapestry and fed it into its own gaping maw, and still it remained unsatisfied, wandering, plundering. A river of a thousand reds vanished, eaten, and it was as if they had never existed. The colour from the whole bathroom began to drain from around her, even white drawn away, leaving an even starker nothing, unlike anything she had ever seen before. Everywhere she looked the colours were being taken away, destroyed and fed into the rapacious machine, leaving a great void in its wake, a void that shot pain through Odette's eyes when she as much as glanced at it.

"Stop it! Stop!" She screamed helplessly at the black hole, but it ignored her words, cheerfully going on about its business of apocalypse. In the back of her mind she heard it whistling, an eerie haunting sound that she couldn't drive away. Whistle while you work!

"Stop!" She screamed again, but it had no more effect than the first time. He couldn't take away her Tapestry, he couldn't. Hasn't he already taken enough away? She slammed her hand into the tapestry, but it felt hard, glassy. She stared at her fingers, realising that they were spread in the centre of a spider-web of cracks in the bathroom mirror. She threw her gaze back to the black hole, but it had disappeared, leaving only a wan reflection of herself. It took her a moment to realise that her hand hurt, her palm was bleeding. She pulled her hand away from the mirror, and a single broken bloodied piece of glass clattered into the sink.

"Shit," she whispered, wrapping her hand in a long sheet of toilet paper. It wasn't particularly adequate, but it would have to do for now. She had to escape the house before the Schillers noticed the broken mirror. She could explain that later, but if they found out now they probably wouldn't let her go out. She peeked out into the hallway, finding it empty. She could hear the sound of the television, which meant that Dieter was downstairs in his favourite arm-chair, but there was no sign of Marie. Perhaps she had run out to a shop or to see a friend. That idea frightened Odette a great deal, but she didn't understand why and tried to dismiss it from her mind. She tip-toed down the stairs, then slid along a wall towards the front door. Dieter seemed fixated by the sensuous glare of the television, unaware of Odette's presence in the room. A moment later she was outside in the cold air, breathing a strange sigh of relief.

Bastian had a car, which enhanced his attractiveness a great deal. It wasn't much, an old red Volkswagen, but it was better than the bus, or walking everywhere. Well, it was faster anyway; Bastian's driving didn't feel particularly safe. Odette sat nestled quietly in the slightly torn-up passenger seat, overwhelmed by a feeling of smallness and an even worse case of shyness. She pushed her back as far as she could into the soft grey cushion behind her, as if she wanted to shrink even more.

"How was school today?" Bastian asked, breaking an awkward silence that Odette hadn't even noticed.

"Horrible," she replied instinctually. Goddammit. She had to learn to think sometimes.

"At least you're honest," Bastian smirked.

"Too honest," Odette said wryly.

"No such thing."

"Honesty only causes pain," Odette quoted Anna darkly.

"It's still better than lying all the time," Bastian affirmed with confidence.

"Why are you so fucking happy all the time?" Odette asked in what she hoped was a light tone. Bastian just laughed.

"I'm serious," she pressed. "I want you to explain the phenomenon of happy people to me. Because I genuinely don't fucking understand what they're so bubbly fucking joyous about. Are you a psychopath?"

"Why would I be a psychopath?" Bastian laughed.

"Well, it's my current theory. People who are happy must enjoy pain, either their own or other people's. So they are either masochists or sadistic psychopaths . . ." Odette realised that she was starting to babble and snapped her mouth shut with a pop.

"You forget blindness and apathy," Bastian replied, with something that vaguely resembled a sober expression on his face.

"What do you mean?" Odette asked. Sometimes she just couldn't help herself.

"Well people can become happy through simply ignoring things or not caring about things. They aren't taking direct pleasure in suffering, they're just refusing to notice it. You can even ignore your own suffering, it's pretty amazing how well people can shut down their brains."

"You're cooler than I thought," Odette replied, with the slightest hint of a smile. It almost physically hurt.

"Well I'm not a complete idiot, you know," Bastian's answering smile was far broader and more noticeable, and for some reason Odette didn't completely hate it. "I'm not just good looks."

Odette giggled, then tried to hide it by chewing on the tips of her fingernails. *Jesus Christ, what the fuck is happening to me?*

"Well, here we are, mademoiselle," Bastian said, not appearing to notice Odette's newly rampant blushing. But he had little chance to see; the crimson colours faded quickly from Odette's cheeks at his last word. Echoes of Rabbit's castigation and stinging criticisms rang inside her mind like a cathedral bell, and for a moment she thought she even saw the strange creature out of the corner of her eye.

"What did you say?" she asked, trying not to sound breathless. That would almost certainly give him a decidedly wrong impression.

"Mademoiselle," he smiled, swinging his car door open. Odette hadn't even noticed that they had parked. "It's French."

"Oh," was all Odette could blandly manage.

"What is this place?" Odette surveyed the small café with its name printed in fancy Italian letters on the window. For some reason it gave her an overwhelming sensation of brown.

"It's a café that my uncle owns," Bastian explained succinctly, opening the door for her in a very gentlemanly fashion.

The dinner was not unpleasant; a very old-fashioned style of date, but Odette didn't mind. It was the first date she had ever been on, she wasn't about to be picky. She tried to remember details so that she could recount the story of it accurately later. Not that Anna would ask, or care. Maybe she could talk to Hilde about it. Maybe

Stefani and Marie were right and having just one friend wasn't the healthiest thing in the world. Especially one as influential and dominating as Anna. Simply having more people to talk to wasn't a betrayal or anything, was it?

CHAPTER 13

puppenmeister

"And how has your sleep been?" Stefani had her scratching pen poised at the ready above the notepad in her lap. Odette hated how interested she always was in the thumping sounds, and simply shrugged.

"Its been alright, I suppose," her tone was barely above a sullen mutter. She could never understand what these people wanted from her. Poking and prying at her brain and scribbling it all down on sheets of paper that they would never read again.

"Do you think you should be on sleeping medication? It wouldn't be difficult to arrange."

"I hate taking pills," Odette wearily traced invisible patterns on her right palm.

"I know, Odette, but you need to keep taking them," Stefani's voice was gentle but unyielding. They had discussed this dozens of times before, and it was always resolved the same way. She was wrong and the system was right. The only way to cure madness was to medicate it into a torpor. Obviously. Why didn't I think of that.

"And how are things with the Schillers?"

This was another question she always asked, but for some reason it took Odette by surprise. She opened her mouth for a moment, but no words came issuing forth. She wasn't good at lying, but something dark inside compelled her to.

"Yeah," she finally stammered, unconvincingly. "Everything is fine there. Marie's great."

For a moment she thought she saw a flash of concern in Stefani's eyes, but then she blinked and it was gone. Just imagining. The office suddenly felt even smaller than it was, as if the walls were bending inwards, trapping them together in an airless claustrophobic pocket.

"Marie called me the other day to express some concern about you. I guess you were having a little trouble discerning reality from dreams on Tuesday morning, is that right?"

Ugh. "It was nothing," Odette scowled. "I just had some bad dreams."

"What were they about?"

"I don't remember," Odette snapped. "I don't want to remember."

"Why don't you want to remember, Odette?" Stefani's voice bore that foxy tone it carried when she thought she was on to one of Odette's cunningly-concealed secrets. "What happens in them that makes you want to forget?"

Is this a fucking game now?

"I told you I don't remember," Odette replied, struggling to keep her tone civil. She couldn't mouth off to Stefani too much, or she might end up back in one of those cute little juvenile mental asylums for crazed delinquents. But sometimes that was very difficult.

"Odette," Stefani said slowly, painted with patience. "Sometimes it's difficult to reveal certain things, but ultimately keeping secrets doesn't help anyone involved. I can't help you if I don't know what it is that's troubling you."

You can't help me anyway. "I really can't remember, Stefani," Odette answered contritely, folding her hands in her lap. "I'm sorry, I wish I could."

"Well, is there anything else you would like to talk about today, Odette?" Stefani asked, placing her pen flat on her paper. She already knew the inevitable answer to this question. To her surprise, Odette paused. Anna.

"No, there isn't anything," Odette finally said, shaking her head after a long moment of silence.

"Are you sure?"

"Yeah."

"Anna and me are gonna hang out here tonight, is that OK?" Odette hung over the back of the living room couch as Marie smoked a cigarette and flipped casually through a fashion magazine.

"Isn't she already here?" Marie asked.

"Well, yeah . . ."

"Then why are you asking me?" Marie laughed, folding the magazine shut. ". . . but it's fine."

"I think it's good," Dieter interjected from his armchair. "Why don't you bring her down here and introduce us?"

"Um . . . OK," Odette said, feeling a tingling of discomfort. And not just because she knew Anna wasn't going to be pleased with this idea, although she had met Marie before. She felt suddenly fiercely protective of Anna, but she wasn't sure what she was protecting her from.

The introductions hadn't gone too badly; Anna had refrained from doing anything shockingly disrespectful, due to Odette's begging. Odette had watched Dieter like a shark for the entire painful duration, and had been disconcerted to find that he was watching Anna the same way. She wanted to say something to Anna about it; she seemed utterly oblivious, but she didn't even know how to begin. She wasn't even sure what she wanted to say. It was there, at the edge of her mind, harrying and worrying at its spiked collar, but there was nothing she could do to drag it under the lamp. Anna sat on the floor, rubbing her treasured knife, which she had smuggled in her backpack, up and down the skin of her forearms. Odette just stared out of the window at a small brown bird perched precariously on the rain-darkened branch that scratched against the glass. Its beady eyes kept bringing back a recurring sense of déjà vu and intense familiarity, almost as if it were whispering things to her just beyond the spectrum of her hearing. It cocked its head back and forth, continuously ruffling its feathers against the downpour, but even as it moved its gaze never seemed to falter from Odette's face.

"Odette? Hello?"

"Yeah, what?" Odette snapped her vision from the hypnotic bird to find that Anna was leaning over her shoulder with a mischievous grin on her face.

"Oh good, I thought I'd lost you for a minute," Anna laughed, tapping the knife blade's flat against the side of Odette's neck.

"Don't do that, shit," Odette gingerly pushed the knife away with her index finger. Anna flipped it around, presenting her with the ornate curved handle.

"I don't want to," Odette protested. "It shouldn't be a fucking hobby, Anna."

"Fine," Anna pouted, dropping the sharp weapon on the bed. "Sure?"

"Yes, I'm fucking sure, goddammit," Odette snapped. "I need to stop that shit or I'm going to get fucking caught."

"OK, OK, Jesus," Anna flopped onto her back on the bed, giggling. "Should we go shopping for tampons then?"

"Oh, shut up," Odette tried to sound stern, but she couldn't help smiling a little and it crept into her voice. "Goddammit."

"Wanna go to L'Affliction?" Anna asked, staring up at Odette's clock.

"No," Odette scowled.

"God, you're no fun at all today."

Odette flopped down on the bed beside Anna, closing her eyes.

"So how did your little date go last night?" Odette's eyes snapped open immediately at Anna's question. Anna hadn't mentioned anything about the previous night all day in school, and Odette had hoped she was going to let it go unnoticed. No such luck.

"It was . . . good."

"Did you guys fuck?"

"No, goddammit."

"Hehe," Anna giggled. "Make out?"

"No . . ."

"God, didn't you have any fun at all? You're turning into such a wet blanket, Odette."

"Look, we just talked and shit, OK?"

"I'm sure he's thrilled with that."

"Oh shut up, god," Odette pushed Anna playfully, and she melodramatically rolled off the bed and landed with a heavy thud on the floor.

"You've turned me into a fucking paraplegic for life," Anna groaned, in between spurts of uncontrollable giggling. Soon Odette started laughing too, as hard as she tried not to, and for a little while it seemed like there was nothing actually wrong with the world.

A strange array of creatures sat around the long oaken table, illuminated eerily by flickering torch-light. Amelia sat at the head of the table, her gloved hands folded passively on the table. Directly to her left sat a tall, sallow man with straw-like blonde hair and an unpleasant expression fixed on his face. This man was Michael, a western human and elected chancellor of the Trifektum High Council. They were both staring fixedly at Odette, who stood nervously at the opposite end of the table, trying to ignore the dozens of strange eyes surveying her with caution and a distinct tinge of fear. She licked her lips, tasting the acrid salt that stood out in strong relief on the soft pink skin.

"What is this?" A hideous creature near the middle of the table hissed. She was huge and bloated, with pasty white flesh that rolled back and forth like seeping mud, supported by eight thin black legs. Dozens of bulbous ebony eyes were set into the swollen body, rolling madly back and forth even as they fixated upon Odette. The creature's gaping beak-like maw was set in the approximate centre of the loathsome mass. A long forked tongue slithered out from between the orange beaks, hovering in the pulsating air.

"This is Alexander's human child, Nayenna," Amelia spoke with a voice of authority that quieted the murmuring that had begun when Nayenna spoke. "His puppet, as some of you here have so perceptively branded her. But a puppet can be worked by more than one master."

"Whatever use you wish to put her to, can she really ever be trusted?" The man who spoke was tall and bald, with skin the colour of cold ash and a pair of huge black feathered wings folded behind his back. But the most striking thing about him was his naked torso, it was entirely covered in softly glowing orange tattoos. Their designs were many; long scripts in strange writing that were constantly subtly shifting and reordering themselves to form a multitude of different words and phrases, strange tribal patterns and illustrations of demonic figures. "Whatever clever and sadistic scheme you've dreamt up for her, Amelia, there is nothing that assures of her loyalty to us and not the oil-sucking fiend."

"What do we have to fear from the birds, Lyneth?" Amelia replied calmly. "Their offensive power is spent as the blight eats away at the core of their race, melting them from the interior. We need hold no anxiety over Alexander's retribution, because there will be none. But while he holds the Tapestry we will never level that cursed hospital to the ground where it belongs. And this . . .

girl knows the location of our sacred Tapestry. This isn't a question of trust, personally," she glanced scathingly at Odette, who remained locked in frightened silence. "I don't trust the little brat in the slightest. I have no doubt that she will try to stab us in the back at the most opportune moment, and then we will have our precious excuse to deal with her."

"Then why wait?" This voice was colder, more chilling, than Lyneth's, but came from the man seated next to him, who looked like his twin. Whether or not he had tattoos was obscured by the spiked black plate armour that he wore, but seemed to bear as lightly as silk. "Let's just torture the brat and get the information from her. What need is there to allow her return to the hospital? Surely we do not require her aid any further."

Amelia laughed lightly. "You darkfeeders are always so eager to torture and slay a human, Mordekai. But we do not need to be so rash. She isn't any good to us dead and I'm reasonably sure I can get all the required information out of her and still keep her alive. She could be an invaluable asset on the inside of the hospital."

"Don't forget who your father was, Amelia," Mordekai answered darkly. The rest of what he intended to say was cut off by a man seated across the table from him. Unlike most of the present company, this man looked altogether normal, Odette wouldn't have looked twice at him on the street were he wearing a t-shirt and a pair of jeans. Which, incidentally, was what he was wearing here. She could have sworn it had been something different a minute ago.

"So we're back to a question of trust . . ." was all he managed to get out before his sentence concluded in a strange popping cough. A moment later his mouth opened wider than Odette thought was humanly possible, and a thin arrow-shaped head came weaving sinuously out, followed by a green and black serpentine body, until half a metre of snake was dangling from the man's mouth. The man's eyes had shut, and his body was relaxed, almost as if he were sleeping. The snake swayed back and forth in the air for a moment, surveying the gathered company with flat black eyes, before swinging around to stare at Odette.

"We were waiting for you, Krysis," Amelia said, leaning back in her chair and lighting a cigar.

"Spit on the angels," the snake replied, its hypnotic gaze never faltering from Odette, who felt an overwhelming surge of fear. "So you don't know whether to trust this . . . human, is that right? Nicholas has been lazy about communication lately."

"The council seems divided," Amelia answered, serenely taking a drag of chocolate-flavoured smoke.

Krysis smiled demoniacally, his black forked tongue flickering in and out of his scaled mouth. "Why didn't you tell them that you plan to steal the Tapestry?" He asked coyly.

"I was getting to it."

"The child hasn't been brainwashed. She is delusional, but it is nothing that would trigger betrayal. She battles inside . . . she is confused by the conflict. She doesn't understand it. It seems that Alexander has plucked her from the lap of true ignorance," the snake spoke quickly, but each word was illuminated with hissing clarity. "But there is another problem with your scheme, half-breed," Krysis whipped around towards Amelia, breaking eye contact with Odette for the first time. Odette staggered as if a huge weight had just been lifted from her back, gasping for breath.

"And what is that?" Amelia asked coldly, significantly less affected by the snake's gaze than Odette had been.

"You will need the Key," the snake answered. "Without it, you will fail."

Without another word the snake retracted swiftly into Nicholas' mouth, and the man's eyes popped open. He ran a hand across his shut lips as if he had just drank a mug of beer, but he didn't say another word. Odette stared at him blankly, feeling transient, lost. She felt unified with him in a bond of sudden muteness; she felt as if she had lost the power to speak, even the power to control the motions of her body. She just stood there, stiff, frozen, like a vandalised statue standing amongst the flames of fallen Rome. The scene around here started to distort strangely, colours mixing where they shouldn't, bits of space swelling up and then shrinking away. Slowly everything started to fade away, all the colours painted over by a bland white paintbrush. The last sensation she got was an alarmed chatter amongst the councillors gathered about the table, and then it all disappeared and she was lying in a cold sweat in her bed, looking up through the darkness at a white clock face. She felt a fluid running from her nose, and when she touched the tips of her fingers to her nostrils the skin turned red. She struggled to sit up, placing her feet on the cold floor. A swimming light-headed feeling overtook her, distorting her bedroom in the same way as the council chamber. She closed her eyes to quiet her churning stomach, but all she heard were Krysis' quiet whispers.

"Find the key, god-child."

CHAPTER 14

schokolade

School seemed like an incredibly unnecessary source of boredom today, even more than unusual. Odette had been oddly untroubled by any sort of hallucination or nightmare all day, and everything was beginning to feel surreally real. Maybe the medication is finally starting to kick in. She tried actually paying attention to what some of her teachers were trying to say, but she soon become overwhelmed with the drudgery of that. What good were mathematics or French or knowing that Otto von Bismarck was born in 1815? Maybe someday they would help her convince the guards of her padded white cell that she was, in fact, sane, and in complete control of her facilities. But she doubted it. Her eyes kept wandering around the class room, waiting for a wall to drip or a bizarrely-coloured bird to come fluttering across the desks, but it never happened. She felt strangely abandoned, alone, scared, sitting secluded in a whirlwind of darkness without a single voice to comfort her.

At least it was Friday again and she wouldn't have to endure this agony for the next two days. Where were her shimmering hallways and calming whispers to rescue her from this mind-numbing normalcy? She didn't feel prepared to face the real world, they had never let her before, an umbrella of insanity to ward away the agonising downpour. Cold, dry, searing facts that couldn't be dismissed as flights of fantasy or tumbling nightmares of filthy darkness. How could she cope with those? It was so simple to shuffle everything painful into the category of imagination, if it was simply not real then there wasn't anything to cope with. Nothing but her sick fantasies. Could real people really be like that? Maybe when she finally found herself pushed out of the darkness of her psyche all she would find is more darkness, stretching on forever and ever and ever.

Why do you cut yourself if you don't think any of it is real?

Because of Anna . . .

She knew it wasn't just because of Anna. She wasn't sure why she was attempting to trick herself on the subject of her own misery, or what the point of that deception was. There was always going to be a part of her that had done the tricking and would always know. Then confusion would just rule her . . . never knowing what was true, what was a trick, what was a lie, what was real and what was imaginary. Maybe an imaginary wrong was still a wrong.

That doesn't make any goddamn fucking sense. If he didn't fucking do it, he didn't fucking do it.

But what if he did?

She wouldn't ever be able to tell, to discern the real from the hallucination, coated with the transience of a wind-troubled flame. Does reality really have any intrinsic value, some elusive worth that sets it above the imagination? Falsehoods, lies, spinning away and towards each other at the same time, none of it would ever come together with logical cohesion. But she had to keep it inside, or she would just become raving madness locked away in a prison of white, spat at and scorned by all the people with their feet firmly planted in their own comfortable realities. None of this was shrouded behind some unreasonably mysterious door, a prison of indiscernible purpose, the ascension of our minds perpetually out of reach. That golden light floating above collective heads, mocking our leaping grasps. So, in time, everyone just looks away, plodding onwards towards eternity, cemented in the comfort of decided truths and lies. Everything shovelled into convenient little orderly piles, so the crowds can pick and choose as they will, content in logic and a four-walled reality.

It will never be that way for you.

And yet the madness had vanished, at least for the moment, dropping her abruptly into this world that she had only viewed from afar. Vague memories of the time before the torment flashed into her mind, when everything had been neat and tidy, precisely where it ought to be.

Never to return.

But what if she could return? Return to that certainty, the knowledge that if you remembered something it was, in fact, true, that it had actually happened. Certainty . . .

Is something you weren't born to experience. Too many chemicals flowing through your brain, overloading the imagery, the sounds, the splashing colours.

And then she could trust again, invested with this new certainty. She could trust, love, work and live like everyone else. It seemed like a fairy-tale, coated in pink and rich white, something that could only be dreamed of and wished after. And yet it wasn't, a cold hard reality, devoid of joy, devoid of wonder, glorified within her mind to the highest of pinnacles, the place of eternal bliss and confidence. Its drabness was the very factor of it that made it so attractive to her. Somewhere that so many colours didn't fly about, dazzling, sparkling, a veritable opiate drugging her into false euphoria. But none of it was real, and thus lay the deception, none of it could be truly valued by the standards of the world. Joy in dreams, pain in nightmares, it was all a convincing hallucination, plastic and fake. A mirror just waiting to be shattered.

"Odette?"

"Odette?"

Odette looked up at Bastian, realising that she was sitting on a bench across the street from their school. Somehow the hellish day must be over. She stared silently at Bastian, slowly realising that he wasn't actually smiling.

"Are you OK?" Bastian asked, before Odette could open her mind wide enough to say anything.

"Yeah . . . yeah . . ." Odette stumbled over the simple words. "I just don't really want to go home, that's all."

"Wanna go out or something?" The boy asked, an endearing hint of shyness in his voice.

"Are you blushing?" Odette teased, standing up.

"No . . . no I'm not blushing," Bastian responded, punctuating his denial with a forced cough.

"Mhm," Odette smiled, hooking her arm around Bastian's. She tried not to let her surprise at her own audacity sneak into her voice. "So where are we off to?"

I need to inject some crack into my fucking brain.

There's nothing to be afraid of. Odette jumped slightly as the front door clicked into location behind her, then she struggled to take a deep breath. Absolutely nothing. Her date with Bastian had gone well enough, she had managed to avoid bringing up any topics that were excessively morbid. She had felt Anna's tight, if not entirely unwelcome, grip start to slip away. And she had yet to see or hear a single figment of her imagination today, which was beginning to nag oddly at the back of her mind. It was almost a worrisome feeling . . . what might be transpiring in her absence, unobserved and uncontrolled? The movements, her Tapestry . . .

"Good evening, Odette."

She almost started screaming at the sound of Dieter's warm welcoming voice, but she managed to swallow it back before it burst into reality. It tasted bitter going back down, an opportunity lost.

"Good evening," she whispered, her voice strained by the fantasy of volume. She looked around desperately for Marie. Why is she never fucking here?

"Would you like to come upstairs, Odette?"

"What for?" This isn't the fucking Odyssey.

"Just do as you're told," Dieter seemed to disappear before he was even finished speaking, the sound of his voice hanging in the empty air. Not one of these dreams again . . . please.

If it's just a fucking dream why won't you tell Stefani?

I don't tell Stefani anything . . .

Shit.

Odette approached the staircase slowly, trembling visibly. Her eyes roved back and forth for signs of the Dream-Dieter, but he was nowhere to be seen. She paused at the foot of the stairs, staring up at the menacing banner of darkness unfurled up above. A dozen voices were screaming inside her head now, but she couldn't discern one from the other, all the cautionary words camouflaged behind a screen of piercing sound. The first step was the most difficult, her feet felt leaden, but with great effort she lifted the right, letting it drop softly on the hard surface of the step.

You haven't fucking conjured all fucking day, why would it start now?

The voice was lost in the rabble of the others, but the warning still flashed within Odette's eyes. She stood on the first step, swaying back and forth, her clammy palm pressed against the wall for support. She collapsed to her knees, vomiting on the fourth, her stomach churning violently. She attempted to struggle back to her feet, but her sweat-drenched body revolted. She began to pull herself slowly up the staircase, her legs feeling crippled, useless.

It's all fucking useless.

It seemed an eternity before she reached the top, her arms and torso convulsed with the conflict. Shit. Her body had moved beyond trembling, it was shaking so violently now that it tossed her thoughts about, her mind a ship on angry waves. Somebody above her cleared their throat cheerily, and she struggled to lift her head high enough to look into the Dream-Dieter's smiling eyes. It has to be a fucking dream.

CHAPTER 15

Verfolgungswahn engel

Finally, a familiar place. Odette stood in one of the dark earthen tunnels of Refuge, fires flickering in mounted braziers on the walls. Earthworms crawled in the dirt around her feet. She peered around curiously in the dancing orange light, but there was no sign of any Trifektum guards.

"Amelia?" she called tentatively, venturing forward down the tunnel. She remembered Amelia telling her that large parts of the complex were abandoned or used only for storage; that must be where I am. Despite the dark, claustrophobic atmosphere, Refuge felt safe and peaceful, the essence of its name.

After about fifteen minutes of wandering aimlessly through the extensive labyrinth, she finally came to a large wooden door, with four iron bars set in a small window, too high for Odette to look through. She tried to turn the handle, a gigantic iron eagle's head, but the door refused to budge. She knocked on it, putting her ear against the wood, trying to pick out the vaguest sounds in the utter silence of the tunnels.

"Hello?" she asked, an unknown influence keeping her voice down to an almost whispering pitch. She thought she could hear the sound of something breathing beyond the door, weak and ragged.

"Hello? Is somebody there?" She heard the sound of feeble movement and sick coughing, a disruption of hay on an earthen floor. She tried to turn the door handle again, to her surprise it rotated obligingly, and the door swung slowly inwards. She peered into the darkness that lay beyond, making out a vague dark figure lying curled on the hard floor. It coughed periodically, a weak, pitiable sound barely capable of life on the clear air, let alone through the caging walls and doors.

"Hello?" Odette repeated, trying to focus on the jerky dying movements of the darkened creature. Its body was half-shrouded in coarse purple hay; Odette could only make out a single eye. It was wide and round, bird-like, with branching black veins marring the frantically revolving pupil. It disappeared for a moment in a long blink, but when it re-emerged it rolled around to stare at Odette, silhouetted in the torch-lit doorway. Odette took a timid step into the darkness, peering at the shrouded shape surrounding the fading eye. The cell smelled horribly, a tainted mixture of death and despair that assaulted Odette's nostrils with brutal force. The dark creature recoiled as she stepped forward, the expression in the eye one of exhausted panic and fear. Disturbed hay scattered into the air, golden in the darkness. Odette froze in place as the captive cowered into the corner, its motions accompanied by a symphony in the rusty scraping of chains.

"Do not be afraid," Odette whispered, kneeling down on the ground. She spread her arms out, palms open and fingers spread, filtering the warm light.

"Child?" The voice that spoke from the darkness was ragged, broken, but it still bore an element, however shrouded, of harsh Metropolitan pride. And it was a familiar voice for Odette, bringing back the whirring roar of engines and the bubbling of oil.

"Lucy? What happened to you?" Odette pulled herself forward, peering down at the pilot's shadowed quivering form.

"Did you tell them?" Lucy hacked, feebly attempting to pull herself up into a sitting position, but failing. "Why are you here, in their fortress?"

"Tell them what?" Odette answered, bewildered.

"You were a spy after all," Lucy's cough had a cynically laughing edge to it. "You radioed them where we were landing . . . they came because of you, didn't they? I should have tossed you out the hatch the moment I saw you. My mother was right, I'm too soft for the military. And you're here now . . . to gloat . . . you needn't be so cruel, I'm dead in a day as it is."

"No, no," Odette protested, waves of guilt crashing over her. "No, please, it's a coincidence, I can't explain it. I didn't tell them anything about you, I wouldn't want this for you. I promise, I didn't. Please don't think now."

Lucy's eye, rolling madly around the cell, fixed itself on Odette again, distrusting and blazing with a new life in betrayal. "What games are you playing with me now, child? If you've come to worm information from me with this ploy, I'm not that foolish. Bring back your whips and your thumb-screws, they were less cloyingly sickening."

"I don't want information from you . . ." Odette pleaded desperately. "I don't care about it. I don't care about this stupid fucking war. I just don't want to see people die or get hurt by it, it's such a waste."

"Then what are you here for? Why are you in their fortress?"

"I don't know why I'm here," Odette answered honestly. "I just find myself places, I can't explain it . . . I want to help you though, if I can."

"You're a day late to bless my grave," Lucy replied with a harsh laugh. "Perhaps I'm going mad, or you're cleverer than I gave you credit for . . . my brain isn't really clicking at full speed right now."

"What's killing you?" Odette pulled herself even closer, so that she could make out Lucy's body. Trembles and spasms convulsed it every few seconds, and thin trickles of oil dripped to the cold floor from her mouth.

"Torture . . . and starvation," Lucy's ragged speech was constantly interrupted by bursts of racking coughing. "Oil is our blood and our water, child. We die rapidly without it, even swifter when our bodies have been agonised for the extraction of information. What have they turned you into, child? Mere children . . . demons . . ."

"They haven't turned me into anything," tears were flowing freely down Odette's cheeks now. "I promise, Lucy, I didn't do anything. I'll talk to Amelia . . . or Rabbit . . . I won't let them do this to you. Please."

"Nothing can help me now, child. I have prayed to Our Lady Odette and Saint Heidi, and neither have heard my petitions. It is their will that I die, so I must accept it."

"It's not Odette's will," Odette protested. "I know it's not . . . I . . ." What if it is? Did I really create all these creatures to kill and destroy each other?

"Give me your hand, child," Lucy coughed, weakly extending a frail withered claw. Odette clasped it between both her palms, fingers intertwined, and held it up to her face, until her tears poured onto the ill grey flesh. Lucy gritted her teeth as the salty water burned acidic on her skin, but she said nothing. But as that pain grew, the rest of it began to fade away, the lingering pain from torture, the racking agonies of starvation and thirst. The black veins standing out in her eyes melted away, leaving them as clear and unblemished as the day she was hatched. Her strength slowly began to seep back into her muscles, her skin darkened to a healthier tone.

"Who are you?" Lucy whispered softly, her voice beautified by awe. Odette's eyes, closed in a vain effort to stem the flow of tears, fluttered open to the darkness.

"What's going on here?" a hissing voice demanded from the doorway. Odette whirled around to find a poison-tipped spear levelled in her face. Its bearer, a grotesquely fat Spider Clan wearing the uniform of a Trifektum guard, scuttled forward a step, bulbous eyes surveying the scene in the cell. His mottled white flesh heaved in disgust as the eyes fixed on Lucy, whom he had fully expected to be dead.

"You, get back in the corner," the guard hissed evilly at Lucy. "You!" laying the flat of the spear-blade on Odette's shoulder. "Stand up and come with me. And no messing about, it only takes a single cut to kill a frail human.

And it's far from painless." Venomous saliva rolled thickly down the creature's fangs as he chuckled.

"What are you doing here? And visiting with enemies of the Trifektum?" Amelia was calm, but a thick undercurrent of fury ran beneath it. She had ran into Odette and the guard in one of the prison hallways, and promptly taken charge of Odette, much to the spider's disappointment.

"I don't know," Odette answered, sitting in a carved oak chair with her hands folded contritely in her lap. They were in Amelia's quarters, ferreted away from the public eye. Amelia did not seem particularly eager to have the other council members learn of Odette's presence in Lucy's cell.

"Listen, child," Amelia said, sitting down in a chair across the table. "Nobody here trusts you. Several of the commanders are advocating your execution, they believe your allegiance to lie with Alexander. I have not yet made up my mind. So, child . . ." Amelia cocked her head oddly in a manner that reminded Odette of a Metropolitan. "Are you lying to me?"

"No," Odette answered softly. Hundreds of thoughts raced madly though her head, but that was the only word she could seem to form coherently. She couldn't explain it to Amelia without sounding like a traitor; she wasn't sure she could explain anything to herself.

"What were you doing with the prisoner?" Amelia demanded, cutting short the flow of thoughts.

"I was helping her," Odette answered automatically. "I don't want anyone to suffer . . ." she stuttered, trying to explain herself. "On either side. It isn't right."

"A little Samaritan, eh?" Amelia's smile was cynical. "Well, it's not for me to say anything. You'll be disillusioned all on your own soon enough."

"I hope not," Odette whispered.

"Well, since you have such a penchant for helping prisoners, perhaps there is something you could do for the Trifektum," Amelia's voice dripped with poisoned honey. "The oil-suckers captured Michael during a raid," she continued after Odette failed to reply. "We have reason to believe that he's being held in the GMK, and we also have reason to believe that he's being tortured for information."

"Just like you tortured Lucy?" Odette asked quietly, slightly shocked at her own audacity.

"Michael is a human," Amelia answered in a slightly bewildered tone. She was silent for a moment, as if that explained everything, before continuing with her analysis of the situation. "We can't let him rot in the hospital cells. The oil-suckers might abandon their own to torment and ruin, but we actually have souls." She circled around behind Odette's chair, placing her cold hands on the back. Her golden archmurderer's ring glinted in the torch-light in the corner of Odette's eye. "If you truly don't wish anyone to suffer," she whispered, leaning down next to Odette's ear. "You won't let the freaks have him."

CHAPTER 16

das vierte reich

Odette's eyes popped open suddenly, the ticking of her roof clock echoing in her mind. For a moment she felt strangely tense, as if somebody were breathing down her neck, but then she relaxed with a rare smile. It was finally the weekend, no more torturous pretensions at academia. The two days where the relentless ticks of the clock were meaningless, save for their dismal march towards next week. But that wasn't something Odette was going to waste time worrying about. Feeling miserable felt so much better when she was free. She lay in bed, staring into the back of her eyelids and attempting to conjure the flowing colours of the Tapestry in the darkness. It seemed like an eternity since she had last seen her Tapestry, and it was beginning to wear on her, a pervasive yearning for another hit, another intoxicating fix. But the shadow-shrouded skin remained dismally blank, devoid of the wonders that Odette so desired. She swung her feet out to touch the floor, swearing softly under her breath.

Less than an hour later she sat with her back against a large blue dumpster, watching Anna spray-paint various obscenities on the side of their school.

"Do you have any cigarettes?" Odette asked, as Anna put the finishing touches on a large red F. Her head hurt, and cigarette smoke always felt so soothing.

"Uh, yeah," Anna replied, pulling a battered and crushed white pack out of her back pocket and tossing it to Odette. "You should help me finish this. A little vandalism is good for the soul."

"I'll take your word for it," Odette fumbled with her light green lighter, which seemed averse to doing its job today.

"I fucking hate this school," Anna complained, viewing her work with hands on her hips.

"Yeah," Odette concurred laconically, closing her eyes and taking in a long satisfying drag.

"Everything's so fucked," Anna continued, doodling a small hakenkreuz beneath the glaring letters. "There, that should piss them off. I wanna watch those pigfuckers scrub this shit off. fucking cunts."

Everything is fucked.

"I mean . . . fuck," Anna hurled the half-empty can at the wall and sat down next to Odette. "I'm so fucking tired of all the same old shit. In, out, like fucking ants crawling around dutifully cause their goddamn queen wants them to. I fucking refuse."

"I keep having these weird dreams about my foster parents," Odette said, in a tone barely above a whisper. She was shocked that she had said it at all.

"What kind of dreams?" Anna had repossessed the pack and leaned back against the dumpster to enjoy her own cigarette.

"Nothing, forget it," Odette answered. Her hand was trembling and she tried to hide it under her jacket. Fortunately Anna was staring up at the sky and wouldn't notice.

"What do you mean, forget it?" She asked, blowing columns of smoke into the blue.

"I can't really remember. I just remember them being weird," Odette stammered, wishing she had never brought it up and desperately hoping that Anna wouldn't press the issue. She had a talent for seeing through Odette's poorly-fabricated excuses.

"I need some fucking drugs," Anna replied, granting Odette's wishes. "Wouldn't that be the best. If I became like this fucking homeless junkie, giving blowjobs for crack money and waking up every morning in a puddle of my own piss and vomit. My parents would be so proud of me."

"I think the prison option is better," Odette giggled. It was difficult not to get sucked in to Anna's cheerful fatalism. If you had to hate everything around you, you might as well be happy about it. It was an outlook that Odette had little difficulty embracing as her own. Why would I want to be rid of this?

"At least if I was a crack whore I would be a free crack whore. Although one could definitely lead to the other . . ." Anna mused, her eyes fixed on the transient smoke, tracing the patterns of such short-lived existence.

"Why are you so sure you're gonna end up in prison?"

"Because I can't control myself," Anna laughed. "You can only get away with that when you're a kid. As soon as I turn eighteen . . . hello bars."

"Cheerful . . ."

"Oh, I met this baldie kid who said he could do a tattoo for me," Anna excitedly cut Odette off. "I'm not sure what I want to get though . . . or where I want it."

"You could get a cross," Odette suggested sarcastically.

Anna laughed acerbically. "Religion is such a fucking crutch. People who believe in that shit just do it 'cause they can't face the world without their precious little divine barrier guarding them from all the filthiness and the fucking evil. The Christians and the camel-drivers are both the same, and they're both so fucking sure of their sacred little fairy-tales that they run around killing everyone who doesn't believe in the same fairy-tale as them. Like I've actually read that Koran piece of garbage and it's just such a load of bullshit. Mohammed was like a fucking schizo, or he was just laughing his ass off when all those camel-driver cunts followed him around like faithful idiotic puppies, believing all the crap he shovelled into their mouths. And he was sitting in his gigantic tent fucking fourteen year olds and just fucking laughing."

"The Christians are almost as bad," Odette interjected quietly, flicking the butt of her cigarette across the cement.

"Oh yeah . . . kill all the fucking Jews, that's the solution to all our problems. And Hitler thought his ideas were original. Church-mandated genocide is the oldest and greatest tradition of Christianity. Hell, I mean even God thought the best way to fix the world's problems was to drown everybody, so what do you expect, you know? Fuck the Vatican. Fuck Mohammed too. And fuck the Jews. Fuck everyone." Anna burst into hysterical giggles.

"Yeah, God's a stupid idea . . ." Odette agreed slowly, watching the gentle breeze toy with her discarded cigarette. Dragged one way then another, spun around and tossed into the wall.

"So what tattoo should I get?" Anna asked, recovering from her little fit of glee. "I think I'm gonna get it on the back of my neck."

"Get a Totenkopf."

"I've been a little concerned about some of Odette's behaviour lately. She's been growing increasingly withdrawn in the last week or so, more resistant to any discussion about her dreams or hallucinations. I'm just worried that something might be upsetting or disturbing her," Stefani's voice sounded slightly muted over the telephone, but still retained her careful therapeutic pace.

"Well, she has always tended to avoid contact with me or Dieter," Marie answered, sitting on a pulled-up dinner chair. "The only change I've really noticed lately is that she hasn't been screaming as often at night, but that's a good thing, isn't it?"

"How anti-social is Odette usually at home? Does she avoid you altogether or does she just refuse to engage in long conversation?"

"Well, it depends," Marie toyed nervously with her white cross necklace. She almost felt as if she were sitting in the therapist's office herself. "She avoids Dieter more than me . . . she won't even make eye contact with him. She will talk with me occasionally, but usually only if she needs to for something. I'm pretty much always a little worried about her, I wish she would be less withdrawn."

"She was abused by men as a small child, which I believe she has lingering memories of, and a general distrust of men may arise from that, particularly if they resemble her abusers in any way," Stefani answered soothingly. "I wish she were less withdrawn myself, but we can't force social behaviour on her until she's willing to accept it, that would just cause her to retreat even further into her protective shell."

"I know, I try not to force any contact on her, especially if she's showing that she doesn't want it," Marie said. "I was a social worker for six years, so I think I do alright at reading the signs on whether or not she wants to talk. I'm just not sure when she's finally going to decide that she wants to be part of life."

"It's very difficult for her. We just have to give her time and make sure that she feels comfortable with all of it. She still has three years before her eighteenth birthday, so we still have time to get her ready for the wolves."

"I can't believe you're asking Bastian over here," Anna complained, withdrawn angrily into a corner of her bedroom. Odette ignored her, staring with fascination at the fire dancing in Anna's picture-framed mirror. They jumped and curled, crackling with simultaneous warmth and anger, repelling and appealing.

"You may be smitten with him and all, but I don't see why I have to deal with the nauseating little pigfucker," Anna groaned.

"Be nice to him," Odette scowled, the fires disappearing to be replaced by her own drab reflection. "Aw, shit."

"What?" Anna's martyred tone was half-interested at best.

"The fire went out."

"What the fuck does that mean, weirdo?"

Odette opened her mouth to reply, but her words were cut short by a soft rap on the closed bedroom door. She sprang with unnecessary speed from her perch on the bed to answer it.

"Be nice," she shot once more in Anna's direction, before opening the door with a demure air of nonchalance.

"Mrs. Schweiger let me in," Bastian smiled in response to Odette's glowing.

"Come on in," Odette grabbed his hand and led him to the bed, where she sat down next to him, a little closer than she had originally intended. What the fuck is fucking wrong with me? Shit.

"Hey, Anna," Bastian raised his palm airily in her direction.

"Fuck you," Anna answered, tapping her forehead three times.

"Goddammit, Anna," Odette hissed.

"I'm sorry, I'm sorry, I'm just kidding," Anna laughed insincerely. "I have a fucked-up sense of humour. Apologies for the many future wrongs I will do you."

"Uh, apology accepted . . ." Bastian answered, darting tentative glances at Odette, who just shrugged. Anna could be a little overwhelming at first contact, he would get used to it. Hopefully.

"Do you have any drugs?" Anna asked, partially emerging from her shrouded little corner, far enough so that Odette could see her eyes staring piercingly into Bastian's skull.

"Does she always say such weird stuff?" Bastian turned to Odette, trying to ignore Anna's predatory glare.

"Pretty much."

"I was born this way, I can't help it," Anna defended herself languorously, stretching out on the floor on her stomach.

"You wanted to be born that way, Anna," Odette scowled. "You probably made God fuck you up."

"God's never touched me," Anna answered, snickering. "That's what my parents think at least. I'm pretty sure they think I'm a changeling or at the very least that my real father is an Incubus. Surely there's no chance something as vile as me sprang from their loins alone."

"I honestly don't know what the fuck she's on about half the time," Odette explained, half-apologetically, to Bastian.

He just laughed, the irrepressible smile re-emerging, which sent a rush of strange pleasure through Odette. A moment later she was kissing that smile, before she even realised what she was doing. It felt good, soft and damp, and she could feel his smile spreading wider.

"Wow, what the fuck," she vaguely heard Anna comment dryly through the excited pounding in her ears. Odette ignored her, even when it was over, she just stared at Bastian with a little smile playing fleeting games on her face.

"Should I go?" Anna continued, blissfully uncaring that nobody was listening to her. "I don't really wanna watch you guys fuck, as comical as that might be. I think I'd just end up hurling and I don't really wanna clean up that shit. And you're doing laundry if you get cum all over my bed cause I don't even wanna touch that shit."

"That was nice," Odette whispered, her arms hooked behind Bastian's neck. He replied by kissing her again, slowly and sweetly.

"Seriously? On my bed?"

CHAPTER 17

rote traum

Odette walked through the sterilised white hallways of the Grand Metropolitan Hospital, a firmness of purpose in her step. Doctors bowed and scraped as she past them, awash in her godly supremacy. She reached the winding staircase that led to Alexander's sacred chambers, and began to swiftly ascend it. Soon she was at his door, a thick steel contraption with a red orthodox cross drawn on it. She knocked loudly, listen to the metallic clanging resound through the staircase and the hallway below. After a minute, with a hiss of steam, the door disengaged from its frame, slowly pulling backwards. Odette walked into the black space, finding herself in a large, red room. The walls were a deep rich red, the furniture and the carpet lighter, softer shades. Even the candles and the books on the bookshelves were red. She walked through the resplendently decorated lobby and through the open door at the far end, finding herself in a smaller room with more modest decorum.

The door swung shut behind her of its own accord, but she paid it no heed. The room she was in now dealt in more bluish hues, a sky blue paint splashed across the walls, and blue and violet decorations; mostly flowers, vases, and ancient tomes. Alexander sat behind a desk at the far end of the room, having cast aside his doctor's coat for his full regalia as High Priest. It was impressive; a thick scarlet robe made of ermine, stencilled with yellow depictions of the three sacred artefacts, the Tapestry, the Pool of Her Soul, and the Key. Thick golden bracelets inlaid with jade, sapphires, and rubies were clasped around his wrists and a thick gold chain set with three gigantic diamonds was hung around his neck. On his head sat a thin crown made of intricately designed silver roses twisted around each other.

"My Goddess," he exclaimed in his croaking voice, hastily standing to his feet and humbly inclining his head. "What brings you here today?"

"Hello, Alexander," Odette said, then decided she might as well go straight to the point. "I want to see your human prisoner,"

"My Lady?"

"You captured a human prisoner, one of their commanders. I want to see him."

"As My Lady wishes," Alexander said. Odette was slightly surprised at his lack of protest. I guess he really thinks I'm a god. He stretched out a claw to ring a bell on his desk. "I will have Oliver, one of my most loyal servants, escort you to the captivity ward."

"Excellent," Odette stated with an air of authority. It was only moments before Oliver, an exceptionally tall

Metropolitan, wearing the standard black doctor's coat of Alexander's elite soldiers.

"Our Lady wishes to see the human prisoner, the commander, that we captured," Alexander ordered him dryly.

Oliver cocked his head quizzically. "My liege?"

"We do as Our Lady commands," Alexander snapped abruptly.

"Of course," Oliver agreed, bowing. He turned to Odette, keeping his eyes lowered respectfully. "Follow me if it is thy wish, oh luminescent one." He turned and headed out of the office. Odette, keeping silent, paced right behind him. It wouldn't do to damage her godly authority with an excess of foolish teenage speech. It was a fairly long walk to what Alexander termed the "captivity ward". They went down several levels, until they were underground. All the walls, roofs, and floors were still painted blinding white, but the area they walked in now had white bars in front of each room and white locks around the white bars. Finally, Oliver stopped in front of one of the larger cells. He fumbled with the lock for a moment, then pushed the barred door open. He stood back, prostrating himself. "Here it is, oh merciful one. I sing thy praise."

Odette nodded curtly and entered the snow-coloured room. What she saw there stopped her dead in her tracks, even as she heard the sound of Oliver shambling hurriedly off.

On the far side of the cell, Michael's naked headless corpse hung from a hook, oozing blood from a multitude of savage tearing wounds. Blood stained the whole cell, puddles of it pooled on the floor, streaks of it stained the walls and even the roof, marring the perfect whiteness. Michael's head lay on the ground beneath the dangling body. His eyes had been gouged out, and his lips, nose, and ears cut off. She could see the bloody little bits of flesh scattered around on the floor as if tossed carelessly aside once removed. He had been castrated as well, the blood-oozing hole in his groin all that was left. She tried to hold back the feelings of sickness that instantly overwhelmed her, but she wasn't able to. She vomited violently on the hard white floor, staining it with green and yellow bile. She stared down at it for a moment, before looking up at the carnage before her again. They had begun to flay him, his left arm and chest were bereft of their skin. The taste of vomit was still on her lips, but she managed to swallow it down before her disgusted churning stomach could cough up another foul delivery. She walked forward into the mayhem, stepping around the thick dark red pools of blood. She could see strips of skin lying around where they had fallen, stained with Michael's blood. She wondered how long he had lived being tortured like that, and how much of it had been done post-mortem out of pure malice. She looked down at the desecrated head; they had shaved all his hair and his beard off as well. Why had they done that? She squatted down to peer at the head more closely. Bruises and welts ran up and down both cheeks and across his forehead, covering his skin in black, red, and purple blotches.

"Can I do anything about this?" Odette whispered to herself. Her feelings of sickness had passed, replaced by an all-devouring curiosity. She vaguely remember stories from the Bible about Jesus resurrecting people. Wasn't she God here? Girl Jesus, she actually smiled slightly. She stretched out her hand over Michael's head, turning it back and forth, feeling the air flow over it. She closed her eyes, and concentrated on her memories of Michael living. She had healed Lucy, surely she could do this. She opened her eyes and stood up, looking over the maimed body. She put her hand mere centimetres away from the bloody corpse, concentrating on what she felt on her fingers, touching her skin. She moved her hand up and down, feeling the cold dry hospital air rush across her palm.

"Where did your soul go, silly Michael," she whispered, stepping back from the body and looking around the blood-spattered cell. She closed her eyes, concentrating on feeling his movement, drifting out there somewhere in the nothingness, probably still in agony from the unspeakable torture.

"Come back, Michael," Odette murmured. "Back to the living. Back to pain." Suddenly she felt something, a strange rush of energy somewhere, almost visible in the darkness behind her eyelids. She turned her head back and forth, trying to get a lock on it, but it skittered around erratically, extremely difficult to nail down. Come back, Michael, She held out a hand over his head, fingers stretching out towards his body, wiggling them in the air. His soul was being drawn back from the abyss or whatever dark place it had gone, she could feel it. Come on. She kept turning her head back and forth. The strange little dot of energy was slowing down, relaxing into a steady orbit of the room. She kept drawing it down 'til it came through the roof, and she could see it sparkling there with her open eyes, a strange translucent light set against the backdrop of red and white. She was starting to feel tired, strain showing in her muscles as they started to ache. She concentrated on her fingers pointing towards the corpse, as one part of her mind held the restless soul in thrall.

Bits of skin and drops of blood began to fly up from the ground, returning to their rightful place in Michael's body. Slowly it built up, more and more floating back into their proper position, healing over scars and the deep wounds inflicted, making the body habitable again. With a curl of her fingers she lifted the head up into the air, setting it down upon the bloody stump of a neck. Slowly she began to repair the head as the last of the gaping gashes on the body closed up. Eyes, nose, ears, lips, hair, all had to be stitched with skin back into their proper place. It was exhausting, but soon she had the corpse back to a presentable condition. She lifted him off the hook, lying him down on the floor. With a flick of her hand she commanded the soul back into the body. For the second the body lay still, cold and dead, but then it gasped loudly and his amber eyes flickered open in shock.

"Breathe," Odette commanded, leaning over him, but not getting too close. "Breathe slowly and evenly." He did as she said, carefully controlling the airflow in and out of him, slowly and steadily refilling his bereft lungs with air.

"Don't try to speak," Odette continued, laying a hand on his shoulder to keep him from impetuously rising. "I wish I could get you some clothes, but I doubt you want to wear anything Metropolitan." The savage look that flashed into his eyes confirmed her opinion, and she smiled wryly. "I guess we can get you something when we get back to Refuge." She looked around the room for a moment, trying to decide how they were going to accomplish this goal. Then she shrugged. Might as well try this. She wrapped her fingers around Michael's shoulder and closed her eyes. When she opened them she was crouching beneath the base of one of Refuge's spreading oaks, and Michael was lying in a bed of soft grass and moss. She looked up to see an armed sentry in a brown cap peering curiously down at her, his gun in his hands. She waved at him, yelling out as loud as she could. "Come down here! We're human! We need help!" He disappeared from sight for a moment, then reappeared with two more Trifektum soldiers, who began to descend the rope ladders. Odette looked down at Michael, who had laid his head back and closed his eyes. "Don't go and die on me again," she teased, then realised he had slipped into a deep sleep. Probably for the best. The sentries were almost down to the ground, so she patted Michael on the shoulder and closed her eyes once again.

This time when she opened them, she was sitting cross-legged on her bed. It was dark outside and her muscles ached, but an elated feeling was racing through her. I controlled it. I did it.

CHAPTER 18

schwatzen

"You have a football match today, yeah?" Marie asked Odette over breakfast. Dieter was at a mate's house, which made everything feel lighter and brighter to Odette. She had barely slept last night, between her excitement over her first kiss with Bastian and the constant thumping of the pole-man outside her door, but she didn't feel as tired as she had expected.

"Yeah," she answered hastily, realising that she had slipped away into a daydream. "Bastian's taking me."

"Who's Bastian?"

"He's this boy I met at school . . ." Odette felt suddenly embarrassed.

"A boy, eh?" Marie's smile was irritatingly knowing.

"Yeah, a boy."

"He's got a car then?"

"Yeah, he does."

"Well that's . . . good," she was probably just relieved that Odette had a friend besides Anna. Boy or not.

Odette felt more comfortable in Bastian's car now, and she stared dreamily out the window as they crept past rows of dingy, shoddily-painted apartment blocks. She would glance at Bastian every now and then with a smile, even though he kept his eyes dutifully on the street. The trip was over far sooner than Odette wanted it to be, but after only a few minutes they were at the field. It had poured rain earlier, and was still drizzling a little, so the already ill-kept field had transformed into a mud-bath. Bastian kissed her briefly on the cheek before she trotted off dutifully to join the rest of the red-shirted girls congregated around their trainer. Hilde gave her an all-knowing look that made her blush and turn her head away, even though a smile spread across the pink.

"Alright, girls," Mrs. Biewer called cheerfully, clipboard in hand. Odette liked her trainer well enough, but the ever-present clipboard always reminded her unpleasantly of sessions with Stefani. She glanced away from Mrs. Biewer to see Bastian crouched against a chain-link fence, his cap pulled down over his face to shield his eyes from the rain. She had difficulty pulling her stare away from him and paying attention as the trainer outlined another masterful plan for the demolition of the opposition.

The first half went well for the Red Shirts, going 3-0 up by the half-time whistle. Odette, despite her significant distractions, even managed to assist one of the goals with a decently-placed pass to Hilde.

"Pay attention, Odette," Mrs. Biewer admonished during the break, despite this success. Odette nodded obediently, but she wasn't sure if she was going to be able to keep that promise. She tried her best to dispel thoughts of the carefully watching boy from her mind, but it still lingered in the corners, springing into view whenever her mind drifted. She felt a little self-conscious, since she was practically covered in mud by this point. As much as she would have preferred not to tackle, she was more afraid of her trainer's wrath if she failed to do so. Mrs. Biewer had a bubbly, pleasant exterior, but Odette was firmly of the belief that every happy person was a hidden psychopath. The second half was a little more bereft, a tall, dark-haired central midfielder named Shianna scoring the Red Shirts' only goal, to neatly wrap things at 4-0. They almost conceded a late goal when Odette let a winger get away from her and hit the crossbar, but the final whistle blew soon after, erasing the chance of any further fuck-ups.

Mrs. Biewer appeared to be too glowingly happy with the result to devote much attention to Odette's mediocre performance, which she was glad for. At least Bastian wouldn't see her get harangued publicly for laziness and distraction, even if it was his fault.

"You're still here?" She asked, trying to sound surprised as he crossed the field towards her.

"Pfft, you were looking at me the whole game," he laughed, his smile growing even broader as Odette blushed deeply. Fuck. "Besides, you didn't think I was going to let you walk home?"

"I'll make your car filthy," Odette protested, gesturing to her mud-caked uniform.

He dismissed this suggestion with an airy wave of his hand. "Its a pile of junk already, what damage could you possibly do?"

Odette just shrugged and followed him at his side, her hand unconsciously interlocking with his. She made a visible effort not to look down at them, but still noticing Bastian's satisfied smile out of the corner of her eye.

"Want to go home or go out somewhere else?" Bastian asked, once they were in the car.

Odette rolled her eyes at him. "I'm not going anywhere looking like this. At least let me get home and change and maybe take a bath before you start dragging me all over town, OK?"

"Agreed," Bastian laughed.

Odette lay in the Schiller's bathtub, submerged in water up to her chin. The mud, which had dried to caked dirt on her skin, slowly began to resume its old form and drift into cleanliness. Bastian had left for the time being, promising to return in an hour or so to pick her up. There was no sign of Marie or Dieter at the house, apparently they had gone out. I might never tell them when I'm going places, but they don't ever fucking tell me either.

"Slightly uncharitable of you," a calm, sophisticated voice sounded from beside her. She ducked her head under the water for a moment in shock, re-emerging a moment later gasping for air, with specks of water clouding her vision.

"No need for panic," the voice continued, as Odette frantically rubbed at her blinded pupils.

"Rabbit?" She stammered, catching a vague glimpse of a svelte suited body standing over her.

"Yes," the horse-headed man replied, folding his hands in front of his waist.

"What are you doing?"

"I was hoping you would tell me that," Rabbit answered dryly.

"Umm . . . I don't know?" Odette ventured unimaginatively, still blinking rapidly to get rid of the last water droplets. Rabbit was not even looking at her, but staring at the cracked tile bathroom wall.

"This place stinks of sin," he observed, in a rather judgmental voice.

"Well, its not my fucking sin," Odette answered, irritated that he would disturb her in this room, of all places. "I don't want you here, so why don't you just go away?"

"If only life were that simple."

"Life is that simple," Odette snapped. "You know, you were much more pleasant when you were stuffed and didn't talk."

"I have no doubt that I was," there was a hint of a smile in Rabbit's voice, even if there was none on his eternally immobile face. "I think that most people would be altogether more pleasant if they never talked, and I am not one to be an exception to general rules."

"God, just fuck off," Odette sighed, considering sinking her head beneath the water's surface again.

"It was very kind of you to save Michael as you did . . . it has conjured a great deal of faith in you among many of the Trifektum's leaders."

"I don't care."

"Ah, but I do," Rabbit answered, that annoying hint of a smile returning to his voice. "How did you manage that trick anyway? It has some of the more cynical leaders . . . quite puzzled."

"Well, they can fuck themselves. And you can fuck yourself too. Fuck off."

"As you wish, milady," Rabbit bowed his head curtly. "But you will be hearing from us again very soon."

With that he exploded into a pile of white ash, which gradually dissolved into the floor tiles. Odette stared at the empty bathroom floor for a long silent moment, before she plunged her head back beneath the water.

CHAPTER 19

Verzerrung

"Wake up, god-child."

Odette's eyes flickered open to the shadows, the words sounding like an echo from a dream, the beginning of the flight of elusive memories upon awakening. For a moment she believed that is what they were, but then she saw Amelia, half-shrouded in the darkness near her shut door. The moonlight seemed to shy away from where she stood, casting only the palest of shadows on her silent cloaked form.

"What?" Odette whispered wearily, still half-asleep.

"It's time to go," Amelia answered in her dead-calm voice.

Odette was still rubbing at her eyes and yawning by the time she stood in Amelia's chamber. The Archmurderer had practically dragged her along a series of winding, dark streets and shadow-infested brambles for a space of time lost on Odette. The only thing still keeping her awake was the annoying stinging pain from the dozens of little gashes she had received from the unkind thorns in their path.

"I would like to thank you for the return of Michael," Amelia stated, as calm and collected as ever, unperturbed and unscarred by the mad rush. She collectively took her seat in her great oak chair. "It was a very generous act, and one that has led us to reassess your value to the Trifektum. But I haven't dragged you from the Nothing to bore you with our grovelling platitudes. As chance would have it, there is another service that I would like to request from you."

"And what's that?" Odette managed to fit in before a particularly long yawn.

"Well," Amelia steepled her fingers together, an aura of cleverness dwelling in the shades of her pupils. "You already know of the Tapestry, and if our . . . ally . . . the Sapphire Werewolf is not spinning me another of his lies, you also know of the Pool of Her Soul. Although, thankfully, you were prevented from looking into it. Who knows what the ramifications of such an exceptional individual as yourself being exposed to that kind of power would be. Especially an individual who persists in keeping the company of Metropolitans."

"What do you want from me?" Odette demanded irritably, blinking rapidly in an effort to dispel the last motes of sleep.

"Those two objects are two-thirds of what we like to call the Three Sacred Artefacts," Amelia continued, unperturbed. "The third is more elusive even than they, although perhaps not as well-guarded. It is called the Key, and it is an object of intense power. It would be invaluable to our war efforts. I want you to bring it to me."

"I don't want to help you with your war," Odette replied angrily.

"Why?" Amelia asked, tilting her head to one side. "Do you think I won't kill you if you refuse? It would, after all, be the most expedient way to prove or refute your god-child claims. And even more intriguing to me is the fact that Sapphire claims to have already killed you. Not that I'm entirely sure I believe him . . . male ego and whatnot."

"You don't believe in the Goddess, do you?" Odette felt her hands beginning to involuntarily tremble as Amelia's murderous eyes glanced up and down her, coolly, calculating. She felt even more frightened of the placid Archmurderer than she had of the gigantic werewolf.

"No . . ." Amelia replied flatly. "No, I do not. Gods and legends for the clergy, I say. If it motivates the masses, then it is a ruse that is worth perpetrating. But wouldn't it be a tad silly for the generals to believe the bullshit that they spoon-feed the ignorant armies? I don't take my orders from any Goddess, or any Tapestry, or anyone who claims to be the voice of the divine."

"Then why do you want to destroy the Metropolitans so badly?" Odette could feel the trembling begin to spread from her hands into her arms, and then into her body. She desperately tried to shut it down, but her nerves seemed unwilling to respond.

"Because killing is what I do, darling," Amelia flashed a wicked smile. "I assure you, as soon as the Metropolitans have been scoured from the face of the world that I will turn on something else to destroy. I highly anticipate a civil war between the Darkfeeders and the Humans once this whole affair is over. And here I am, a half-breed, caught in the middle of it. My, my, which side should I choose? Whose blood will be sweeter for me to drink in?"

"So that's all you care about?"

"It is, love," Amelia calmly drew her flintlock pistol from her trench-coat and laid it on the table. "As long as I live, there will be no peace in this world. And I seriously doubt that situation will change when I do inevitably die."

"So why should I help you?" Odette stammered, the shaking reaching her face, chattering her teeth madly together.

"I thought I made it clear that I wasn't negotiating," Amelia's expression was quizzical. "I want the Key, so you will bring it to me. Consider it an order."

Odette opened her mouth to reply, although she hadn't the vaguest idea what she was going to say. But she was interrupted before she could speak, by the appearance of two large figures looming out of the darkness. They stopped either side of Amelia's chair, two werewolves, one tall and black, the other short and ashen grey. Neither of them were as impressive and imposing as the Sapphire had been, but Odette felt a new chill of fear nonetheless. Not that she thought Amelia needed their help in dispatching her, if that was her desire.

"This is Mirk," Amelia suavely indicated the black werewolf on her left.

"And this is Pit," gesturing at the grey. "They are the . . . assistants of the Sapphire in keeping his eternal duty. His lieutenants, if you will."

"What do they have to do with me?" Odette challenged belligerently.

"Well, they are experts on the Three," Amelia replied. "You don't expect to rush headlong to the Key and just take it, do you? It will end as unfortunately as your encounter with the Sapphire."

"I never said I was going to get the Key," Odette said stubbornly.

"Do we have to go over this again, darling?" Amelia's smile was deceptively motherly this time.

"The Key is located in a cave atop the highest mountain in the world," Pit interjected before Odette could even open her mouth to reply. His voice was low, harsh, and guttural, like bones rattling over each other.

"It is guarded by a Keeper as ancient and powerful as the Sapphire," Mirk continued, almost as if it were the same person speaking. His voice stood in sharp contrast to Pit's though; it was dark, silky, and cold.

"The Key is kept near the back of the cave," Pit picked up flawlessly. "But whether or not you are victorious against its Keeper is entirely on your shoulders."

"Good luck, child," Mirk's voice flowed like an ice-cold stream as both werewolves faded into the darkness like clouds of unholy mist.

"Will that be enough to help you find it?" Amelia taunted.

"Yes," Odette's voice was cold, frozen anger. "It will."

CHAPTER 20

Vogelbad

Odette's tapestry hadn't changed in the days since she had seen it last, and it overwhelmed her with the enticing aromas of its own addiction. Pink and grey and dozens of shades in between cascaded down from the roof and vanished into the sucking mud, already long forgotten as Odette widened her eyes and drank in the wonders of her own creation. There was nothing as beautiful, as entrancing, as this marvel that had sprang from the wells of her own imagination. She stood transfixed before the crashing waves of colour, hardly daring to blink lest she miss a vital shred of emotion.

"Its beauty will never fade with time," Alexander's ragged voice sounded at her shoulder, the harshness of it tempered by respect and awe. "An eternity of wonder, a gift granted to each generation in their turn," he continued, his own eyes never faltering from the Tapestry's message. "It is our duty to protect it, from whomever would rob the descendants of the Metropolitan race of their birthright."

"If there even is a Metropolitan race," Odette answered, unwilling to look towards Alexander as she spoke. "You're dying out, aren't you?"

"We will never disappear completely," Alexander smiled, his gnarled claws folded inside his sleeves. "Don't fret for us, little goddess."

"Because I'm going to be your saviour?"

"Precisely."

Odette turned away from the Tapestry now to look at the Metropolitan high priest. His head was cocked to the side, surveying the colourful display with clinical detachment. "How do you know I can do that?" Odette demanded. "Days keep passing and I never feel any more like this goddess you claim I am."

"You resurrected the human prisoner, didn't you?" Alexander asked, almost mockingly.

"You killed him," Odette snapped. She continued to stare pointedly at the Metropolitan, but his gaze never once faltered from the Tapestry, so consumed by his hypocritical homage.

"Yes, I did," Alexander replied calmly, no trace of remorse in his tone or face. "I have killed a great many people, sometimes the fatal blow, at others simply the fatal word. But it is all the same. Without my existence they would still exist. And perhaps, if I had permitted them to exist, it would have meant the end for me. And so the world spins on, unconcerned with the bloodshed and the massacres, just existing. Our existence is the only thing that matters, yours, mine, any person's. I do not begrudge my enemies the right to battle for their own spark of life, nor do I think they are evil for doing so. But neither do their deaths plague my dreams, their dying whispers ring in my head. I feel no regret, no remorse, for the things I have done, because they have all done for the greatest cause of all, existence. The value of each person's life is, of course, highly relative. No life is as important as your own, and despite high words of morality, you will find that everyone is the same in that respect when they are pushed to the brink."

"Then why do you kill them? Why do you fight them?" Odette asked, the Tapestry behind her paling and turning into a lacklustre mixture of light brown and dirty white. "Couldn't you just live in peace with them, and then everyone's existence would be preserved."

"Well," Alexander smiled, almost fondly. "The mistakes of my youth continue to haunt me, and will doubtless do so until my grave. In those days I was greedy, and consumed with a lust for power. I had to crush the ant-like races surrounding us under my iron heel, and make them grovel in the mud, I felt compelled to do so. I had to burn their temples, destroy their homes, slaughter their children, and, of course, rob them of their most sacred relics. And now they will never forgive my race, or me, not in the space of a thousand years. Red blood burns hot in their veins, passionate and angry, and the coldest of them, the ancient Darkfeeders, never forget an injustice done to them. They will make sure the other, more transient races of blooded people never forget either. The stories will pass from parent to child for generations until they become nothing more than legends and myths. But I have found it takes far less than a legend to doom an entire race to the fire."

"What if they would forgive?" Odette plead. "What if they would forget it, leave it all behind them, admit that everyone makes mistakes."

"Some miracles are even beyond the gods, my child," Alexander replied, a clouded, faraway look shrouding his pupils.

"Odette? Odette? You there?" Odette's eyes flickered open to find Anna leaning over her, snapping her fingers. "Oh, good, I thought you might be in a coma for a second," Anna said, a wicked smile playing on her lips.

"Where the fuck am I?" Odette groaned, rubbing blindly at her eyelids. "Goddamn, it's too fucking bright."

"Umm, we're outside our school," Anna replied, digging through Odette's bag. "School is over, in case you hadn't noticed."

"What the fuck are you doing?" Odette demanded grouchily, grabbing the bag away from Anna.

"Fine, be a wet blanket," Anna responded cheerily, standing and slinging her own bag over her shoulder. "But I had a chat with your little boyfriend and, if you're done being a total bitch, we're going to his cousin's place to get wasted. So, wanna come?"

"What?" Odette squinted against the bright rays of the sun. She felt like she should still be in the cool, dark Tapestry chamber. "What the hell . . ."

"It's OK," Anna said reassuringly, as she began to strut off. "I'll just tell him you weren't feeling well."

"Wait, wait . . . fuck," Odette moaned, staggering unevenly to her feet. "Why is the sun so fucking bright today?"

"It isn't."

It was only a half-hour walk from the school to the house they were headed to, but in the opposite direction from Anna and the Schiller's house. The neighbourhood was quite a bit worse than theirs; thin stray dogs wandered around the streets, prying curiously at calmly drifting litter. Anna had to fend off a pushy homeless beggar with a savage tirade that made Odette cringe. They finally got to the building that Anna claimed contained the apartment they were seeking. It was a squarish concrete construction, covered in ancient white paint that was peeling off in dozens of places.

"He told you his cousin lives here?" Odette asked, as Anna forged ahead, pushing open the iron-gated door.

"Mhm."

Odette faithfully followed Anna as she navigated the narrow bare hallways and the cold flights of stairs. For a terrifying moment she wondered if Anna would vanish in front of her, leaving her alone in this horrible place.

"Here we are," Anna chirped, stopping at a white door with the numbers 521 painted unconvincingly in black upon it. She rapped sharply on the door, four times. "They better have vodka," she murmured.

The door swung open, to reveal Hilde standing in a barren hallway, her blonde hair hanging loosely around her shoulders instead of in her normal braid.

"Hilde?" Odette asked somewhat stupidly, as if the answer to her question weren't standing in front of her.

"Hey, Odette, how have you been?" Hilde smiled warmly, easing Odette's surprise.

"You know her?" Anna asked suspiciously, casting dark glances back and forth between the two of them.

"Yeah, yeah . . ." Odette murmured. "She plays football with me. I didn't know you were Bastian's cousin," she continued, to Hilde. "You didn't say anything to me."

"Yeah," Hilde beamed. "Come in, come in, don't stand out in that awful hall."

"Bastian!" She yelled, as soon as they were inside the apartment. "Odette's here!" The rock music that had been blaring deafeningly from one of the rooms cut away suddenly, and Bastian's cheerful face popped into line of sight. He hugged Odette, conservatively, as Anna dropped down in a wooden rocking chair.

"So where's the shit," Anna asked brazenly. "I came over here to get wasted."

Hilde disappeared into the apartment's small kitchen, giggling. She emerged a few moments later, a tall cold bottle of Russian Standard vodka in each hand.

"Drink up, Odette," Anna giggled, as Hilde handed her one of the bottles. Odette looked at it with slight distaste for a moment, she had never drank alcohol before and hadn't really the slightest idea what to expect. Painfully aware of Anna's shameless encouragement of delinquency, she tipped the bottle up and took a quick, if cautious, swig. For a moment she didn't taste anything, then the strange heat of it hit her throat, along with the acrid after-taste.

"Good, isn't it?" Anna asked, taking a somewhat excessive chug of the remaining bottle.

"Jesus Christ," Odette puckered her lips. At least it made her belly feel warm. Hilde had disappeared again, this time to reappear with two more bottles, one of which she passed to Bastian.

"Cheers," Anna laughed darkly, clinking her bottle against Hilde's.

The night grew progressively stranger for Odette, both darker and more colourful, fragmented like a jigsaw puzzle. She remembered kissing Bastian's neck as he stared off blankly at something in the night, Anna and Hilde dancing wildly to loudly blasted europop, and then collapsing on a thread-worn couch together. She remembered kissing Anna, as the older girl laughed, pointing at shadows playing on the wall. She remembered a gigantic snail crawling through the room, leaving a thick trail of black slime behind it. She heard Alexander's voice, murmuring indistinct fragments of wisdom, and Bastian's, loudly singing a song in a horrible off-key. She remembered Hilde tripping over the edge of the rug and falling heavily to the floor, and then just lying there laughing for the next twenty minutes. She remembered skulls dangling from blood-stained chains in the air, and then, finally, she remembered darkness.

CHAPTER 21

heilige krieger

"Fuck!"

Odette sat bolt upright on Hilde's bedroom floor, dishevelled and disoriented. The first thing she realised was that all her bones were aching horribly, but then again the floor wasn't terribly soft. The second was that it was an hour after noon.

"Fuck, fuck, fuck, fuck," she whispered rapidly under her breath, staggering unevenly to her feet. Anna, curled up against the still-slumbering Hilde on her bed, opened her eyes painfully, before rolling off the bed and landing with a muted thump on the floor.

"Ow," she muttered, rubbing her hands against her arms. "Wow, the fucking sun hurts."

"Where the fuck is Bastian?" Odette demanded shrilly, looking desperately around the room.

"Oh, he left . . . like after you passed out I think, or something," Anna was rubbing her head now, moaning.

"I don't fucking know, everything was spinning by then anyway. Why, you guys shag?"

"Its fucking Tuesday, we're supposed to be at fucking school," Odette couldn't seem to cut the volume of her voice, but Hilde slept on like the dead.

"Who gives a fuck? I mean, come off it, Odette," Anna groaned, lying prostrate on the floor. "Does it really matter?"

"Shit," Odette sighed, sinking down to her knees. "We're going to get in so much fucking trouble."

"What're they gonna do, execute us?" Anna giggled. "Who cares?"

"I have to call Marie. Can i have your cell phone?" Odette's mind was running rapidly now, desperately searching for a way to get out of this.

"I don't know where the fuck it's gone, to be honest."

"Goddammit, Anna," Odette half-screamed, frenetically scrambling about the room in search of the missing phone. She finally found it pushed beneath Hilde's dresser, wrapped up in a blue jacket. She fumbled at the number-pad for a moment before finally getting Marie's number.

"Hello?"

"Oh my god, Marie, hi," Odette stammered, as Anna rolled her eyes on the floor.

"Odette? Where the hell have you been?" Marie almost shouted. "We've been worried sick about you. Stefani just called us and let us know you weren't at school and you haven't been at home since yesterday morning."

"Yeah . . . I know," Odette whispered. "I'm gonna come home now."

"What the fuck is going on?" Hilde groaned.

"You can't just run off and leave us like that!" Marie's voice had calmed somewhat, but it was still more than a little strained, as she paced back and forth in front of Odette, who sat on the couch with her hands folded contritely in her lap. "You have to think about other people sometimes, Odette. If you want a new foster home, you can just tell us, or tell your worker."

"I don't . . . I don't want a new home," Odette whispered into her lap. "I like it here, I really do. I'm sorry."

"Were you with Anna?"

"Yeah . . ." Odette muttered, after a lengthy pause.

"Jesus Christ," Marie collapsed into Dieter's chair with an exasperated sigh. "I won't bar you from seeing her or anything . . . but, please be careful, Odette. Anna is not a good influence, and we both know it."

"She's my friend," Odette's muted voice took a vague streak of rebellion.

"I know, Odette, and I'm not saying you shouldn't hang out with your friends or whatever, just . . . we worry about you when you just disappear. And we could get in a lot of trouble, Odette, we're your legal guardians. If you really want to stay here like you say . . . do you really want to put it into jeopardy and get taken away from us? They will do it, Odette, they really will."

"I didn't realise," Odette stammered, a tear creeping into the corner of her eye. She brushed it away quickly, hoping that Marie hadn't noticed. If she did, she didn't let on.

"Come on," Marie stood up again, brushing a hand across Odette's shoulder. "I have to take you to see Stefani."

"So what were you doing last night?"

"Nothing," Odette slouched angrily on Stefani's little couch.

"Well, it couldn't have been nothing, Odette," Stefani leaned forward slightly, an annoyingly reassuring smile on her lips. "You missed school this morning. A little truancy isn't something that would normally cause immense concern, but you're not exactly a normal case. Can you remember what went on last night?"

"Yeah . . . up until I fell asleep," Odette murmured, staring at the wall.

"So what happened?"

"Does it fucking matter?" Odette snapped. "I went out, I drank a little, and I missed school. That's it."

"I'm just concerned about an increase in your anti-social behaviour, Odette," Stefani's smile faded to be replaced by a sterner expression. "A certain amount of it can be expected from someone in your position, but you've never gone this far before. What's changed?"

"Nothing has fucking changed," Odette hissed through her teeth. Stefani was really pissing her off today. "I made a fucking mistake. Aren't I allowed to do that or am I suppose to be fucking Jesus Christ now?"

"Of course you're allowed to make mistakes, you're human just like anyone else," Stefani's voice had shifted again, this time for an ingratiating tone. "But if you decide to go absent without notification again you're going to be suspended for a short while, and that decision is out of my hands, OK?"

"OK," Odette grumbled. "Can I go now?"

"Not quite yet," Stefani flipped open her notepad, pen poised at the ready. "Did you have any peculiar experiences while you were intoxicated?"

"Nothing that I can remember," Odette sighed. She felt tired.

"Interesting . . ." Stefani murmured under her breath, scratching down far more than Odette had said. "How are things at home?"

"Well Marie isn't exactly pleased with me right now, but other than that everything is fine."

"And your relationship with Mr. Schiller?"

"What the fuck do you mean?" Odette snarled, suddenly revitalised.

"Well, you live in the same house, surely you have some sort of functioning relationship with the man."

"I have no fucking relationship with Mr. fucking Schiller," Odette ground out.

The flash in Stefani's eye was altogether too piercing for Odette's liking, and she immediately began to fret over whether she had let on too much. What the fuck is she gonna draw from that anyway? Bitch.

"OK then," Stefani said slowly, her wan smile restored to her fake face. "I'm sure you're very tired, Odette. I'm going to let you go now . . . take a nap and look after yourself, please."

CHAPTER 22

der schmied

I can't explain these things I see, these things I suddenly know, appearing to me as if a sudden mist had lifted. This is my world, I created it, I rule it, and somewhere in the deep vaults of my mind I know all of its secrets. Sometimes I have to dig, long and painfully, but in the raw flesh everything is buried, and in time I will know everything that I was born to know. Everything that I, in some ancient time and unknown dimension, created.

"This is the place," Odette gestured with the flickering ashwood torch she held in her left hand. "I know it."

Rabbit turned his immobile eyes on her for a moment, before gazing into the black depths of the cave. They were almost to the top of an enormous mountain, its side littered with boulders three times Odette's height. She approached the cave mouth slowly, holding her torch out in front of her at arm's length. She could hear a familiar sound ringing out from the abyssal depths of the cave, echoing among the rocks and boulders on the mountainside. The steady thump-thump-thump that plagued her sleep every night, but many times louder; she could hear a metallic clang shivering in the middle of the repetitive sound. Her first reaction was to clamp her hands over her ears and sink to the hard ground, but she fought that back, gritting her teeth and attempting to swallow her fears. Resolutely she took a step forward, then another, and another, until she was standing inside the swallowing darkness of the cave. She could hear Rabbit's even breathing behind her as she pressed forward into its stone-studded, yet softly welcoming throat. Droplets of water fell shimmering in the darkness from menacing stalactites dangling from the cave's roof, landing with soft touches in small dark pools.

Odette picked her way through the jagged stones and menacing stalagmites that peopled the uneven cavern floor. The air was thick and smothering, pulsing with the sounds that tip-toed through it: the hiss of the torch, the water-drops, Odette and Rabbit's gentle breathing, and of course the menacing thumping, which grew louder with every footstep that Odette took. It did not take the darkness long to swallow up the pitiful remnants of sunlight that attempted to illuminate it. Soon the only light remaining emanated from Odette's steadfast torch.

"Did you hear that?" Rabbit whispered, and a tremulous note of worry had crept into the cultures of his normally emotionless voice. A moment later the change dawned on Odette, and she tried to fight back the strange fear that suddenly surged through her soul. The thumping, which was so familiar to her now that it readily sank into ambiance, had stopped. A moment later her feet, which had continued the mindless motions of moving forward, came to a sudden halt, and Odette held up her hand for Rabbit to do the same.

"There it is," she whispered, the pervasive fears fleeing from her thoughts, if only for the moment. She pointed at a brilliantly shining object that lay across a stone alter thirty metres in front of them. It was a sword, with a long blade made of sparkling sharpened steel, one side smoothed and the other notched and jagged. The straight unadorned guard was iron, and the grip was wrapped in oiled black leather. The pommel was a jet black oval stone, so smooth and dark that it reflected images around it like a mirror. Odette started running towards it, as the fears returned, driving her legs forward with their uneven rhythms. Seconds later, she stood before the altar, looking down at the Key, which seemed to shine with a light of its own. The altar was covered with strange etchings; drawings of destruction and warfare and peculiar symbols that Odette couldn't comprehend. She reached a trembling hand out for the Key's handle, stopping just as the edge of her fingers brushed the leather.

"Who has the arrogance to lay their hands upon the Key?" A bellowing voice rang out, reverberating with crushing force against the shadow-covered cavern walls. Odette's fingers wrapped around the handle, squeezing so hard that her fingers turned red. The blade rose in the air, as light as the proverbial feather, the magnificence of its lustre increased a dozen times. The speaker came striding through the darkness towards the empty altar, dust rising from around his leather-booted feet with each gargantuan step. It was a gigantic man, wearing nothing but a filthy brown rawhide smock. He had short sharp grey horns jutting from the sides of his bald head, and a dark black beard that did little to hide the twisted angry expression that consumed his face. A huge livid red scar ran from his forehead into his beard, crossing over the puffed socket that use to contain his left eye. He carried a gigantic mallet with a steel head in both hands, his enormous knotted fingers curled tightly around the black oak handle.

"I will crush you into dust and forge your bones into weapons, foolish little girl," the man bellowed harshly, hefting the gigantic hammer with a malicious smile spreading across his pock-marked features.

"Who are you?" Odette took a half-timid step forward, brandishing the Key in her right hand. She could see Rabbit retreating back towards a cavern wall, always the pragmatist. "Are you the one outside my door?"

"I stand outside a thousand doors," the man boasted. He did not look at all intimidated by Odette's steadfast posture. "I beat my hammer, my soul, against my anvil from sunset to sunrise every night, and rest when the cursed sun torments the earth. I have no name, I am only the Blacksmith, the forger of the Key at her holy behest. And I am tasked to destroy any foolish one who so much as looks upon the key, and here you have laid your pretentious mortal hands upon its unfathomable steel. I suppose I shall have to take . . . an extra amount of pleasure in my duty."

"These hands are not mortal," Odette responded in a challenging tone. She held the Key in front of her, trying to remember what she knew about sword-fighting from the few movies she had seen which contained it. She had a feeling it wasn't going to help very much.

"We shall see," the Blacksmith said, quieter than his normal tone, before suddenly rushing towards her, bellowing a strange war-cry at the top of his lungs. Odette stood frozen in shock for a splinter of a moment, before evading his first blow, a crushing strike that came sailing down from above. It crashed into the rock floor, sending chips flying in every direction. One struck Odette across the forehead, leaving a bloody gash. She staggered as the Blacksmith whirled around with disconcerting speed for one so large, sweeping his mallet towards her side. Odette threw herself to the ground, feeling the powerful blast of wind as it rushed over her, striking nothing but air. She scrambled swiftly back to her feet, desperately attempting to regain some form of equilibrium as the towering monster came at her again, wielding his sledgehammer. She ran towards the altar, sharply aware of the soft sound of her shoes slapping against the stone. The Blacksmith leapt after her, launching his gigantic frame through the air with a powerful thrust. Odette dodged to the left just as his hammer came crashing down on the altar, shivering the ancient edifice in half with a single blow. For a moment his side was exposed and Odette sliced wildly at it with the Key. The magnificent blade slit through his rock-hard skin as if it were nailed paper, and he let out a shrieking howl of pain, clutching at the blood-spouting wound. Dark red seeped through his knotted fingers, trickling onto the ground. Odette took a few faltering steps backwards, staring at the mayhem she had wreaked. The Blacksmith only remained in shock for a moment, then he rushed towards Odette again, his hammer whistling in the darkness. The blood sprayed freely from his wounded side, but he didn't appear to care. She slipped quickly to the right, the point of the Key sliding across the Blacksmith's ankle, leaving a thin bright trail of red there. He collapsed to one knee, his hammer clattering to the ground, free-falling from his limp fingers. Odette tried to shut out his anguished groans, but they pierced through her pale hands, delving deep into her suddenly guilt-ridden mind. She almost tossed aside the Key and rushed to his side, but some inner inhibition held her back. The Blacksmith staggered back to his feet, leaning down slowly to bring his mallet back to bear.

"Please stop," Odette whispered, holding out a hand. "I don't want to hurt you."

The Blacksmith snorted derisively, gaining more sureness with each step he took. He wielded his hammer above his head. "I cherish the pain," he growled, charging towards her again. This time Odette's daze did not fall from her swiftly enough and the mallet's blow struck her squarely in the stomach, sending her flying backwards against the stone wall of the cave. She landed gasping on the ground, bruised and aching from the force of the blow. She heard his footsteps ringing vibrantly in her head as he came striding slowly towards her, draping himself with all the pomp of an executioner. She staggered slowly to her feet, the world spinning chaotically around her. By some miracle her grip on the Key had not been broken, it dangled limply at her side. She raised it slowly, trembling, as the Blacksmith bore down upon her, each measured menacing stride bringing him closer. He swung the hammer in the air, a horrible smile spreading across his hideous features. Odette jumped to the side just as it came crashing down on her head. She thrust desperately at his stomach, wincing as it buried itself deep in his soft organs, greedily lapping up his flowing blood. The cadence of the Blacksmith's groans seared themselves into Odette's mind, the pitiful whimpering death-song of a demon. His gigantic cooling corpse crashed to the floor, reverberating for a moment before lying still, his steaming blood pooling around his dead flesh.

Rabbit approached the corpse, dead plastic eyes placidly taking in the scene of carnage.

"Well done, mademoiselle," he remarked calmly.

"Well done?" Odette stammered, glancing in disbelief from the horse-headed man to the dead creature lying in a puddle of hissing blood.

"Well done?" Her voice rapidly rose several octaves, peaking shrilly. "He's fucking dead! What the fuck do you mean, well fucking done?"

"You did not imagine that you would be able to acquire one of the three sacred artefacts without destroying its guardian, did you? That would be quite impossibly naive . . . even for you."

"Oh, shut it," Odette hissed, wearily letting the Key's tip rest against the stone ground. "Come on, we better get this fucking thing back to Amelia."

"You'll let her go."

"Why?" Amelia, comfortably seated at the head of the otherwise-empty council table, folded her fingers together, eyes quizzically and somewhat suspiciously surveying Odette from head to toe.

"Because I'm advising you to do so."

"Maybe you would like to advise me on how exactly releasing a prisoner of war without any recompense whatsoever is in the Trifektum's best interest, eh?"

"She's going to fucking die," Odette snarled, leaning forward over the far end of the table. "What use is a dead fucking prisoner to you?"

"A hell of a lot more use than a live Metropolitan," Amelia answered calmly.

"Your recompense can be my continued co-operation in your little war. I brought you your precious little weapon, didn't I?"

"Your motivations continue to elude me," Amelia's took on a slightly bemused tone. "If I were like my somewhat dim-witted colleagues I would also simply question your allegiances, but I am not that simple. I know that they don't lie with us, but I also know that they do not lie wholly with the Metropolitans either. So where do they lie? Are you such a simpleton that you think you can play both sides to your own advantage? Such an endeavour can only result in scorched fingers, I assure you."

"Her release is the only payment I want," Odette reiterated stubbornly.

"Well . . . as you wish I suppose," Amelia shrugged. "It does seem a terribly odd favour to ask though."

"Don't worry about my motivations. I . . ."

"You don't know them yourself?" Amelia cut in. "That doesn't really surprise me terribly. Still, your very existence . . . remains somewhat of a mystery to everyone. Even to our occasional friend the Sapphire Werewolf, and I can't recall anything else that was a mystery to him."

"Just release her . . ." Odette didn't feel like responding to a battery of insinuated questions that she had no answer to. "You'll release her, OK? I want your promise."

"You have my word as a murderer," Amelia half-smiled. "I'll set Lucy free."

CHAPTER 23

paranoia

"You are with us, aren't you?"

Odette looked up from her quiz paper to see Alexander's stooped form looming above her, supported by a skull-tipped cane. There was a sharp look of inquisition in his strange eyes, strained and exhausted, but still calculating. She glanced around the school room, the silence only broken by the busy scratching of pencils, each student slumped laboriously over their desks. She looked back down at the paper, loaded with innumerable questions that she hadn't the slightest understanding of.

"I mean, I know very well who you are," Alexander settled himself wearily on the edge of her desk, his hands folded over the grinning skull. "But I am beginning to question if you yourself have full knowledge of it . . . or if you fully appreciate it. Infused with the divine, there is still a very human weakness about you, and perhaps, a primitive instinct to seek out others of your species."

Odette did her best to ignore him, dutifully filling in circles at random on her quiz sheet. When she looked up again he had disappeared, but there was still a heaviness in the room, crushing down on her. It grew slowly stronger, until the pressure against her chest was stealing her breath and forcing her to gasp. She didn't even notice all the curious eyes turn in her direction, her own hands at her throat, trying in vain to fend off the calmly compacting weight. She thought she heard Alexander's voice whispering through the darkness that swam in her head, but she couldn't make out the words. Softly, like a mattress, the weight crushed the life from her broken body, and she lay twisted and flattened upon the floor, watching her soul drift to the roof, imprisoned inside a purple balloon. Her soul pushed her ghostly hands and nose against the thin rubber cage, peering down at her old prison of flesh, cooling on the floor. Her eyes flickered shut, their purpose fulfilled, their journey complete. The balloon drifted through the ceiling and everything slowly faded to black, her body, all the curious students gathering around it, water dripping from the edge of the desks.

Odette sat picking listlessly at her lunch, staring off into nothingness. Anna wasn't here, she wasn't sure why. Perhaps she had another therapy appointment keeping her out of school, or her parents had finally gone insane over their daughter's bad behaviour and murdered her. They would probably chop her up and feed her to stray dogs or bury her somewhere deep in the woods.

"Hey," Bastian slipped into the chair across from Odette, his smile a little faded.

"Hey," Odette replied, her voice lacklustre. She pushed a hunk of bread listlessly around on her plate with a metal fork. She wondered if it would burst into flames out of anger, but it just there, dull and dry and crusty.

"I'm sorry about last night," Bastian began awkwardly, mindlessly watching Odette swirl her food around her plate. "Um, I . . . um, I didn't mean it to be quite like that, I guess. I didn't want to get you in trouble anyway, I know. I should have taken you home or something, I'm sorry."

"It's OK, it was fun," Odette answered, glancing down the side of her chair as if she expected a dog to be begging expectantly there. She looked up at Bastian, who was almost sweating out of nervousness. "Where did the dog go?"

"Umm . . . what dog?" Bastian asked, responding as if the oddness of the question hadn't quite registered.

"There was a dog here. A little brown mutt. I think there was a dog, anyway," Odette looked on the other side of her chair and then turned around to peer over the back. "Where the hell did it go?"

"This is a school, I don't think there was a dog in here," Bastian said, trying to keep the blatant puzzlement out of his eyes.

"Yeah, there was a dog," Odette assured him, peering under the table. "It had like scraggly fur and a long face, I think it was a stray or something. You know, like those dogs that always hang out with the bums and steal food from them."

"I think somebody else would have noticed if there was a dog, Odette," Bastian tried, and mostly failed, to sound soothing. "Why don't you just eat something, eh? Lunch looks pretty good today."

"Are you serious?" Odette asked, her head popping up above the table again. "It's absolute shit. It's absolute shit everyday, and I'm used to it, or I'd be puking all over the floor right now. That's how shitty it is. And I'm not hungry enough to eat shit today."

"Just trying to be positive," Bastian murmured, digging away at his own food with no compunction.

"Where did that fucking dog get to?" Odette whispered to herself, continuing to swivel around in her chair and peer around different tables, trying to catch a glimpse of the elusive mutt.

"There's no dog in here," Bastian reiterated hopelessly, perfectly aware that Odette was barely hearing him.

"It's gotta be around here somewhere," Odette murmured, slipping out of her chair and wandering aimlessly around the large open room, tilting her head from one side to another to glance around visual barricades and bustling students. Bastian shrugged at his empty plate as Odette faded from his line of vision, before dragging hers across the table.

"Hello?" Anna's petulant voice was withering, even over a telephone line.

"Where were you today?" Odette demanded, sitting on the edge of the Schiller's kitchen table. She hadn't seen Bastian again the rest of the school day, but then again, she hadn't been looking for him.

"My parents took me to see Dr. Krasinski again," Anna hissed. "They called me in sick 'cause of Monday night. It was bullshit."

"How did that go?"

"Fat old bastard poked and pried and scratching his fucking bald head for a couple hours, before making up a bunch of random shit about me and spewing it to my fucking ignorant parents. And they lapped it up like stray dogs, of course," Anna's voice, despite its venom, had a distinct tone of resignation about it.

"How many times are they gonna keep you out of school for that shit?"

"Fucked if I know. Fucked if anyone cares. Fuck it all," the line went dead at the end of this outburst, but Odette just shrugged and hung up the phone. She was used to Anna's tantrums.

Odette found herself standing in a shallow river, wide and calm and placid, the rippling water gently running past her ankles. Everything beyond the river was hot sand, stretching as far as she could see. The sky was blue, bright and cloudless, the dot of yellow sun spreading its wealth generously to the earth. She turned slightly to look behind her, the serene water disturbed by her movement. There were four palm trees lined up in a perfect row a dozen metres from the edge of the river, but they stood completely still, no wind, no sign of life about them. Odette looked down at her wet ankles to see that the crystal blue water around her was darkening, until she was standing in a tiny pool of pitch blackness amongst the beauty of the river. Slowly two tiny streams flowed from her pool towards the centre of the river, arcing out as they picked up pace and then coming together a stone's throw away from her. For a long moment nothing happened, everything seemed as perfect and calm as the moment she had stepped into this dream. She thought she heard the music of a bird far away. Then something reared its head from the beautiful waters, a long sinuous dark grey shape. Two blistering red eyes appeared in the darkness, fixed with determination upon Odette, who stood rooted like a tree.

The figure leisurely unfolded itself, a wide menacing hood either side of its flat, arrow-shaped head. The jaws sprang open like a trap-door, revealing two long curved fangs, green acid dripping from them into the river. The water boiled and hissed as each venomous tear-drop struck its peaceful surface. The creature began to slither through the water towards Odette, darkness spreading out from its long slender body. She stood like a statue, transfixed by its entrancingly evil eyes. They held no mercy, no remorse, no emotions, such darkness and beauty melted together. As she stared at them the colours began to flow, black, dark red, purple, and violent orange, the shades of her Tapestry channelled through a demon. They seemed to grow in her mind, until she could no longer see the creature that carried them, all her thoughts consumed by the intoxicating opium of the Tapestry.

But it only flickered for a moment, and then it was gone, replaced by the searing pain of two fangs piercing the skin of her exposed leg. She staggered back a step, looking down desperately into the water, but the creature had disappeared into a cloud of black smoke. Agonising pain shot up her leg, twisting and convulsing her stomach, constricting her chest, closing her windpipes. She clutched frantically at her throat before sinking to her knees in the river, the poison stripping her of the strength to stand. All the water had turned black now, tossed by some unseen storm, wrathful and confused. Destruction and pain surrounded her, the four trees caught fire, her dimming eyes could only find more scenes of death and carnage, no matter where they turned. And then she fell sideways into the welcoming waves, and cold darkness swallowed everything up.

CHAPTER 24

erschrockene engel

Odette's eyes snapped open suddenly, focusing on the ticking black clock-hands set in white above her. One hundred. Why the fuck am I awake? She was physically exhausted from football training, her legs ached from all the running, but her brain buzzed actively, rebelling against the peaceful slumber that lurked on the outskirts of her imagination. The darkness sat thickly above her, calm and sedate but still vaguely menacing. Something about staring into pitch darkness had always disturbed Odette, as if it were something she oughtn't be looking at. The complete silence weighed heavily on her mind as well, she never would have dreamt she would actually miss the repetitious pole-thumping that terrorised her nights, but now something seemed forever missing. He was dead, and he would never come back . . . in retrospect the steady sounds that had kept her frustrated and sleepless on so many nights now seemed like a lullaby. A songbird shot in the mouth.

She didn't even notice her door swinging gently open until after Dieter was already in the room. She stared at him in silence for an eternal agonising moment, her brain refusing to process his dark presence. I'm fucking dreaming. I have to be asleep. He swaggered towards her bed, a wicked smile idly playing on his satisfied face. She sank deeper into her bed, her frozen fingers fumbling with the edges of the covers. Her brain desperately wanted to scream, but her constantly-straying mouth failed to respond to the urgent messages. Dieter sat down on the edge of the bed, pulling the covers out of her limp grasp and peeling them away from her shivering body. His rough hand caressed her face, pausing as they brushed over her lips, a finger gently inserted over her tongue.

"Good girl," he whispered, leaning down to kiss her on the cheek, and then dragging it across her trembling mouth. "I knew you always loved it."

"Stay the fuck away from me," Odette hissed toothlessly, the venom fleeing from her voice.

"Now don't be like that, love," Dieter answered, sliding the edge of Odette's night-gown over her shoulder. "Marie's asleep in just the other room, you know."

"I'll scream," Odette faltered. An idle threat, all the air seemed to have abandoned her lungs.

"Sexy," the man replied, his plundering hands taking bolder liberties as his eyes locked Odette's in. "It won't do you any good though, I took a few liberties with sleeping medication in her night-glass. But we both know you wouldn't anyway, you want this."

"No, please," Odette whispered, tears trickling at the edge of her eyes. "Please."

"It's your own fault, you know," Dieter continued, ignoring her pleas. "There's only so much a man can resist before he breaks."

Odette wanted to push him away, but she felt overwhelmed with the helplessness of it. He was so much stronger than her, struggling was futile, he would just hurt her again. "Please don't," she whispered again, not that begging would be any more effective than physical resistance. His hands were on her legs now, taking their lustful time, enjoying her weeping weakness. She felt like a rabbit in the headlights of a car, frozen and hypnotised by the fear and beauty of imminent death. She could scream for Marie, even if she could muster it, but the cries would fall on deaf slumbering ears, intoxicated with near death.

"Too bad I don't trust you enough to stick it in your mouth," Dieter whispered, exploring fingers at her slit now. "You might feel like taking a little snap at it. Feisty little thing. It'll come in time though. You're already so much more obedient."

He pulled the edge of her night-gown up over her hips, leaving her legs and hips naked and exposed to the darkness. "How would you like my cock in your mouth, eh, love?"

Odette spat at him, rather inaccurately, as it landed on his left shoulder. Dieter just laughed, grabbing her around the neck and constricting, cutting off the already weak flow of air to her lungs. "Now, come on, behave, little bitch," he chuckled, as Odette's lips parted in desperate search of oxygen. He released her suddenly, leaving her gasping helplessly as he sat back and pushed his strained boxers down. He hooked his fingers around the edge of her panties, pulling them down to her knees. She felt intensely open and vulnerable, as if her skin had been flayed from her bones and the blood was trickled out from open veins.   "No more spitting now, or I'll have to really punish you," he whispered in her ear as he slid himself inside her, chuckling more at her shocked gasp at impact. For the first time she was certain that this was no hallucination, it felt too real, too devastatingly painful. Dieter's tongue traced snake-like patterns on her cheeks and around her ears as he continued his unchecked assault, over and over again until Odette felt as if she would burst from the invasion. She stretched her arms out behind her head, resisting the natural reaction to hook them around Dieter's neck. She couldn't encourage the sick bastard, she just couldn't, she wouldn't. This is fucking real, you fucking liar.

Odette felt herself floating in the air. When she looked down she couldn't see her feet, or feel her hands. She was an incorporeal entity, drifting through nothingness. The GMK stretched out below her, rows and rows of white beds. Off to the east she saw a strange flash of red, on one of the walkways that ran on the hospital walls. In the space of a moment she was beside it. Amelia was there, dressed in black, with a black hood covering her hair. One telling strand of it fell down her face, caressing her cheek. She had a hard, determined look in her blue eyes, a look that made Odette remember her title. Archmurderer of the Trifektum. Odette tried to call her name, but she had no mouth with which to do so. She watched helplessly as Amelia lay a suitcase down on the metal grid of the walkway and entered its password. Click, click, click. The lid popped open to reveal padded foam wrapped around shiny black metal tubes.

Amelia pulled them out, quickly and expertly screwing them together. Murderer. In a matter of seconds the assassin held a sniper rifle in her hands, which she rested on the guard rail of the walkway. Odette looked across the hospital, across the vast sea of white beds. Alexander stood there, at the doorway to the Tapestry, so far away that Odette could barely see him. Amelia screwed the scope onto the top of her gun, and peered through it. Odette was beside her now, she could see the cross-hairs hovering on Alexander's wrinkled forehead. He just stood there, looking out over his stricken people, praying . . . praying to me, Odette thought. And here she was, unable to do a thing. Amelia's black-gloved finger rested on the trigger now, as she shifted the barrel back and forth. She had all the time she would need for her nefarious act. Odette could hear Alexander's prayers echoing through her mind.

"O mighty goddess, lady of the night, lady of mercy, we, thy humble people, thy humble servants, beseech thee to stretch forth thy hands of mercy and plenty. Touch us with healing, fair goddess, touch us with thy love. Vraktiz gevelnez Aastathru vu bedlethek immeldrath. We prostrate ourselves before thy judgment, hurling ourselves into the abyss with only thy net to catch us. We lay all our faith, all our pain, all our devotion, at thy feet, and thy feet alone. Please, Odette, I beg thee on my knees for my people. We are in desperate need of thy mercy."

A shocking crack split the air. All the white-coated doctors prowling between beds looked up from their charts as the noise ripped across the hospital. At the

Tapestry door, a thin black line of liquid splashed onto the white surface. Amelia's aim was flawless, a deadly bullet piercing Alexander's brain the merest flash of time after she pulled the trigger. As soon as his body hit the ground she was in action, throwing the sniper gun down on the ground and running off down the walkway, pulling a small black pistol out of her coat. Odette followed her as she ran at incredible speed. She could hear the sounds of chaotic shouting, panicked orders being issued to the Metropolitan Guard. It wouldn't take them long to find the place she had fired from.

Amelia ripped open a white door and headed down a spiralling staircase, vaulting over railings until she reached the bottom in a matter of seconds. She shot off the padlock on a door at the bottom and kicked it open. Odette could hear the clatter and loping run of the Metropolitans coming down the staircase. Amelia ran out into the Hospital Gardens, and Odette knew that she could hear them too. She dodged through trees and shrubbery, pulling a small hooked knife from her belt. Then Odette saw what she was running towards. Lucy's airship, all its propellers whirring frenetically, sat in a fountain courtyard, its outer door sitting open. Two Trifektum soldiers sat in the cockpit.

A Metropolitan Black Coat burst through a thick screen of brushes, standing between Amelia and the airship, his sword upraised. His death was instantaneous, Amelia didn't even stop running. She evaded his powerful strike with the swiftness of a serpent, burying her knife in his jugular vein. She was in the airship before his corpse hit the ground, the knife's white handle still protruding from his neck. A stream of oil pooled on the ground.

Amelia slammed the airship door shut and it took off vertically from the courtyard pavement, its four legs retracting into its belly. Gunshots rang out as several more Black Coats burst onto the scene, but they were too late to do anything but mourn their fallen comrade. The airship whipped around in the air and was off, bullets ricocheting harmlessly off its metal hull. Odette felt frozen in shock by what she had seen. Her own High Priest murdered before her eyes, and she had been helpless to stop it. Couldn't or wouldn't? A quiet voice whispered in the back of her mind. How could she be helpless here, where she was God? Everything was slipping away from her, so fast she wasn't even sure what she was losing. How . . .?

CHAPTER 25

rosa weltall

Something had compelled Odette to bring a knife to school. She had been sitting on her bed, toying with it, watching the blade flash as she spun it around, when she had suddenly slipped it into her bag. For a long moment she had just stared at the handle sticking out from amongst the other junk, then she had brushed some papers over to hide it. Her walk to school had been disrupted by constant visions of death and chaos. Bleeding corpses strewn about the street, mutilated and mangled by some unseen force rampaging through the city, screaming animals fleeing down the pavement. Headless bodies staggered about, drenched in their own spewing blood, unwilling to accept their inevitable fate. The sound of large iron chains dragging painfully across the concrete resounded through Odette's head, mixed with devilishly hysterical laughter.

She sat in the far back of geography class, desperately attempting to concentrate on the major cities of Australia, but mostly failing. She kept darting glances about, catching horrifying images out the corner of her eyes. Blood dripping from the wall to her left, pooling thickly on the ground. A flaming skull flashing across the front of the class-room, giggling like a psychotic young girl. Burning acid bubbling out from the ground beneath her feet, popping and hissing.

Odette collapsed inside a stall in the school bathroom, tremblingly extracting the knife from her bag. She held the handle gingerly with two fingers, watching the blade as it swung back and forth, like a clock-hand gone insane.

"Dear blood, what is this?"

Odette looked up sharply to see the crouching Sapphire Werewolf looming over her, a sharkish expression on his face but a sad, longing look in his eyes.

"This is the girl's bathroom," she stammered weakly, painfully conscious of his hot breath in her face.

"I'm androgynous," he replied, lolling his tongue out.

"What do you want?" Odette demanded, feeling a sudden surge of confidence, even as she attempted to conceal the knife behind her back.

"There are many things that I want. But they really don't concern you as much as what you want. Or what you need, in some cases."

"You killed me once," Odette challenged, the knife slipping from her fingers and clattering on the floor.

"Well you needn't have any fears on that," the wolf practically laughed. "You were invading my privacy then, but you seem to have rebounded from the experience quite well, if I may say."

"You're invading my privacy now, so do I get to kill you?" Odette replied belligerently. Her numb fingers desperately searched behind her back for the renegade knife.

"I doubt it," the wolf answered, but there was a surprisingly introspective gleam in his eyes. "But you are a god-child apparently . . . after all . . . so what you do and do not get to do seems beyond my authority to dictate."

"Well, piss off then," Odette's fingers touched the edge of the handle and she dragged it screeching across the cold floor until she could wrap her palm around it.

"Now that I'm afraid I can't entirely do," the wolf answered, rocking back on its haunches. "Dear blood, you aren't going to try and attack me with that little blade, are you? You don't even know that I'm real."

"Does it matter?" Odette asked, lying the knife down in her lap.

"Not particularly. And you did succeed in killing my compatriot the Blacksmith, so perhaps I should not be so confident, despite the result of our last encounter. It seems that god-children grow rather exponentially."

"Your compatriot?"

"Why, yes," the wolf smiled, a predatory smile that Odette couldn't bring herself to trust. "The guardians of the three sacred artefacts are all in league. I was friends with the Cardinal before Alexander killed him and despoiled the Tapestry. Now only I remain, my artefact the only untouched wonder in the world, the others lie desecrated, exploited for their power."

"But I thought you were allied with the Trifektum?" Odette's eyes wandered around the claustrophobic bathroom stall. Air seemed to whistle and vanish around her ears.

"Well, I quite prefer them to Alexander and his unnatural race, but I have my own purposes. Allegiance or no, I would no sooner let Amelia and her motley crew of rebels near the Pool of Her Soul than I would Alexander's oil-suckers."

"I see," Odette whispered.

"Said the blind man," the Sapphire Werewolf laughed.

"Can you go away now so I can cut myself?" Odette asked. "I don't like doing it in front of people . . . not even Anna."

"As much as I would love to oblige, I'm afraid that I can not," the wolf replied solemnly.

"Go away," Odette scowled. The wolf just sat on his haunches and stared at her calmly, his eyes transforming into deep pools. Colours began to rush down across them, mimicking her beloved Tapestry. They were dark, angry, brooding colours; bruised purple, black, storm-cloud grey, shadow-cast red.

"What the fuck . . ." Odette whispered, leaning closer to stare into his compelling eyes.

"You see what you need to see," the wolf spoke in a trance-like monotone, devoid of any emotion or inflection. Odette was only centimetres from his blade-like fangs and warm lolling tongue now, consumed by the shifting painting in his eyes.

Suddenly she blinked, and he was gone.

Odette sat silently on Stefani's small couch, still filled with the feeling of intense emptiness that had struck her the moment the wolf had disappeared. She wanted answers so desperately, but everyone who seemed to have them hid behind such an impenetrable mist that it was beyond hope for her to ever find them.

"So how have you been feeling today?" Stefani began with her typical drab question, pen poised above the ever-present notepad.

"What? Sorry . . ." Odette shook her head as if it would help shake the clammy spider-webs that clung so persistently at the frayed edges of her mind. Everything felt shrouded in fog now, answers, facts, lies, misinformation. She couldn't sort one from another, lost in the thickness.

"How have you been feeling?" Stefani repeated patiently, scribbling down some note before Odette even opened her mouth to reply.

"I haven't," Odette whispered, looking down at her lap. She half-expected her knife to be lying there, obediently waiting until its mistress wanted to use it.

"Come again?"

"I haven't been feeling . . . not today, anyway."

"Have you felt numb? Disassociated?" The pen was madly scratching now.

"No . . . I haven't been feeling. At all. Not one little fucking bit. I wish I could still feel fucking numb at this point."

"Odette?" Anna gingerly pushed open the cracked door of the Schiller's house, poking her head inside to peek around.

"Odette?" She repeated, in a slightly louder voice.

"Oh, hello . . . Anna, is it?" Dieter emerged from the kitchen, wiping his hands on a dish-cloth, a friendly smile on his face.

"Uh, yeah," Anna answered coldly. "Is Odette about?"

"No, sorry," he replied affably, draping the dish-cloth over his shoulder. "She's still at her appointment with therapy. She should be home shortly though . . . you can come in and wait for her, if you like."

"OK, yeah . . . i guess sure," Anna said darkly, eyeing Dieter with innate distrust. She never trusted adults.

"Would you like a drink?"

"Have some beer?" Anna settled herself down on a couch in the living room, wrapping her arms around her bag.

"I'll get you a coke," Dieter replied, laughing and disappearing into the kitchen. He reappeared a minute later, the black drink sloshing in a red hard plastic cup.

"Cheers," Anna toasted half-heartedly, accepting the proffered beverage. Dieter settled down in his arm-chair, watching her with hawk-like intensity as she sipped slowly, looking suspiciously around the cosily middle-class room.

"You're pretty good friends with Odette, yeah?"

"I'm her best friend," Anna snapped in reply. "Her only real fucking friend, actually."

"Well that's good," Dieter smiled. "Marie and I care a great deal about her, you know, although she can be very withdrawn most of the time. It's good to know that she comes out of her shell with at least one person."

"Well she wouldn't have to come out if she hadn't ever been stuffed in there in the first place."

"I suppose you're right," Dieter leaned back in his chair, studious eyes never faltering from Anna. "We hope we can correct some of the damages of the past, with enough nurture and support, anyway . . . it might be a big ask, but harder things have been accomplished with enough effort, you know."

Anna opened her mouth to reply, but she was cut off as the room started to keel to the left, rolling unstably like a ship in a storm. She blinked several times, trying to bring it back to a state of normalcy, but all the colours began to mix together, drab white in drab brown amongst the corner-lurking blacks. Her stomach began to lurch violently and she fell forward from the couch onto her knees on the floor, arms wrapped defensively around her clammy belly.

"Fuck is this . . ." she forced out, vaguely aware of Dieter's large shadow looming directly above her. "You fucking pervert, don't fucking touch me."

She fell forward on her hands, hacking emptily at the floor, even as she felt his hands wrap around her inert body. "Fuck . . ."

CHAPTER 26

feuerzeug

Odette sat on Anna's front porch on Saturday morning, slowly puffing on a cigarette and watching her friend out of the corner of her eye. Anna seemed oddly subdued today, speaking in a quiet, unobtrusive voice, her words lacking their typical brazen streak of obscenity. Neither of her parents were home, they were visiting family in Geltendorf. She was staring silently off into the overcast sky, her eyes unexplored like mysterious pools.

"Is everything OK?" Odette finally proffered timidly, shifting her gaze nervously back to the curling smoke drifting around her head. She felt the brief sting of the tendrils touching her eyes, but she tried to ignore it. Anna didn't answer her for a long moment, and when she finally spoke it was with a measured and careful tone that seemed grossly unfamiliar.

"Want to make a deal with me?"

"What kind of deal?" Odette was wary . . . something strange was going on here, but she couldn't put her finger on it.

"Well . . . what would you do if I killed myself?" Anna's head suddenly snapped around so that her blazing eyes stared straight into Odette's.

"Do you want to kill yourself?" Odette stammered, taken aback by the burst of ferocity.

"Why shouldn't I?" Anna sighed, the fires flickering out. She turned her eyes back to the dreary fog oppressing the freedom of the sky.

"What do you want me to do?" Odette snuffed the remnants of her cigarette out on the concrete.

"Kill yourself with me," Anna laughed tersely. "I think I understand suicide pacts now. It's a lot easier to go if you know you're not going alone. Probably what motivates mass murderers too."

Odette stared with wide eyes at her friend. It took a moment for her to realise that her mouth was hanging open slightly and she hastily closed it with a slight pop.

"Come on," Anna's voice still had a laughing edge. "You don't want to make me become a mass murderer, do you?"

"What's wrong, Anna?" Odette felt tears springing to the back of her eyes. "Why do you want to kill yourself? Please . . ."

"Oh come on, don't be a baby," Anna snapped. "The question is, why don't you? Oh . . . it's that little fucker, isn't it? What's his fucking name? Torsten?"

"Bastian . . ." Odette was almost cringing at Anna's acid-stained assault.

"You can't fucking trust that little piece of shit," Anna was hissing like a demon. "Come on, how can you be so goddamn blind? He just wants to fuck you, you stupid little bitch. He wants to fuck you, and then he's going to move on to some other stupid cunt and fuck her. He's a fucking man, don't you get it? I thought you were too smart to fall for this kind of pig shit. You can't trust him, Odette, OK? Look at me, goddammit."

Tears were flowing down Odette's cheek, spattering on the grey concrete. She looked up at Anna's face, contorted into some unearthly illustration of fury.

"Listen to me, Odette," she said, her tone softening. "You can trust me, OK? I would never want to hurt you, you have to trust me." Her hand reached up to stroke the side of Odette's face, gently brushing the tears away. Odette's lips trembled, but she couldn't force any words out, her larynx locking up in confused rebellion.

"I don't want him to hurt you," Anna's voice shook, and Odette knew she wasn't talking about Bastian. "I don't want anybody to hurt you." A moment later their lips were touching, the faintest moist caress that sent shivers down Odette's spine. The ticks of the clock echoed in Odette's mind a hundred times before she pulled away, her head dizzied by the cloying smell. She staggered to her feet, the world spinning strangely around her. For a moment she expected it to transform into the Tapestry, but it just kept shimmering in eternal transition.

"I'm going to go home," she whispered quietly, looking down at the ground. She turned around and walked away quickly. Anna sat motionless and watched her go, a thousand struggling screams locked inside her soul. She wanted to run after her, to stop her from walking back into that monster's den, to scream all the warnings her head burned with, but all her muscles had melted into water. Helpless trickling water.

The tiny plume of flame danced to the imperceptible movements of the air, mesmerising Anna's eyes with its flowing grace. It flickered against her skin, filling and overflowing her nerves with a rush of agonising ecstasy. She wanted to drown everything in pain, to sear the broken gates of her mind shut with the cleansing fire. The scent of scorched flesh barely registered in her nostrils as she pressed the lighter against her leg. A dark ashen circle marred her pale skin, a tattoo of her addiction. Screaming, she hurled the lighter at her bedroom wall, watching it clatter to a rest on the floor. A faint trail of smoke rose questioningly from her leg, before disappearing forever into the black light. Anna lay curled on her bed, staring catatonically at the inert lighter lying on the floor, cold and lifeless without her touch. No more knives, no more fires, no more fucking crying.

None of it seemed capable of fortifying the flood-gates that withered and cracked, weakening with every passing moment. In her mind she saw an unending parade of therapy, drugs, sparkling white coats bearing needles in their false hands. Was there really any more point to going along with this pathetic farce of life? The experience of emotion, the experience of feeling, of love . . . hollow, empty, useless. It brought nothing and gave nothing, all it did was strip away from her soul, piece by piece, until she was consumed by the nothing left behind.

God, angels, devils, they were all the same to her now. Every one of them an emissary of pain and destruction, raining down their edicts and commands upon her unwilling heart. An act of life, an act of lust, was there a difference? Simply existing, weak, helpless, torn by the claws of the world, acted upon for pleasure and pain. And it wasn't any more wrong than eating ice cream. Why would anyone subject themselves to this, living in a world of hopelessness and despair when there was such an easy road of escape? So soft, so mortal, so breakable, the delicate shells that guard our eternal souls. Preserved like rabbits, profligate propagation that submitted our seed to the same horrors we have already experienced. An act of pure selfishness, but wasn't that all that mattered? Yourself . . . yourself . . . yourself . . . fuck this. All I need is a time and a place.

"Thanks for coming," Odette said softly, giving Bastian a swift peck on the cheek and a wan smile.

"Is everything OK?" he asked, a worried look creasing his carefree brow. Odette had called him and asked him to come over without really explaining why.

"Let's go somewhere," Odette replied evasively, tugging at his sleeve. "I don't want to stay here."

"OK, babe," he said, forcing a smile for her sake, although worry still nagged at the back of his mind. Odette was amazed that she could have ever hated that smile, and she nestled her head under his arm.

"So what's going on, then?" He asked, once they were already in the car.

"It's Anna . . ." Odette replied slowly, unsure of how to explain it properly. "I don't really wanna talk about it."

"That's fine," Bastian smiled again, soullessly. There was a part of his nature that was very empathic, and he could sense the deep disturbance in Odette's soul, even if she didn't admit to it. "Wanna go out somewhere?"

"Can we just go to your place?" Odette asked, rubbing her forehead.

"Sure."

Odette laid her head wearily on Bastian's shoulder, curled up next to him on his bed. His parents weren't at home, they were out to dinner somewhere.

"She's my best friend," Odette whispered. "She's the only friend I've really ever had. She just gets so . . . crazy, sometimes, I can't deal with it."

Bastian stroked her hair soothingly, fiddling occasionally with individual strands. "She'll come around," he said, sounding more confident than he had a right to. He barely even knows her. "Whatever she's mad about, she can't stay mad forever, yeah? I think you're as important to her as she is to you."

"I don't think anything's that important to Anna, really."

"Nonsense," Bastian answered cheerily, mussing Odette's hair. "Everybody has things that are important to them."

"Anna isn't everybody."

"She'll come 'round," Bastian whispered, softly kissing Odette on the top of her head. She tipped her face up so that he could kiss her on the lips, and she was on her back before she hardly realised it. Bastian's arms were around her shoulders as he passionately kissed her, the smell on his lips intoxicating. She started to kiss back, feeling his soft tongue pushing between her lips. She wrapped her arms around his neck, letting herself be carried away on the winds. He smelled so very, very good. His hands moved down to her waist, fingers slipping inside her pants. They felt cool and soothing against her skin. His hands curled under her shirt, pulling it up over her head and outstretched arms as she giggled. I hope this isn't a dream.

Moment later, Bastian's shirt was tossed onto the bed alongside her own. Odette ran her hands over his lean torso as he unbuttoned his jeans and pushed them down, still kissing her softly on the lips. She lay back on the bed as he crawled on top of her, an oddly innocent boyish smile playing on his face. She unfastened her bra, sliding her arms through and tossing it to the side.

"You're beautiful," Bastian whispered, kissing her lingeringly on the side of the neck. Odette just smiled, her brain scrambling for words to say, but failing. He pulled his boxers down, and his naked body lay over her, pushing her gently down into the bed. His fingers toyed with the waistband of her panties, before sliding them slowly down her thighs. She was exposed again, and for a flashing moment there was a world of darkness filled with unblinking eyes, but then it faded as rapidly as it had been born. His warmth pressed against her, seeking and touching. Her skin felt hot, but she felt cold inside, her stomach filled with bitter ice. Bastian continued to kiss her lips, but now they didn't respond, dead and frozen. Then he pushed inside her and with an agonising sear the idyllic moment melted away. She smelled Dieter's rancid breath on her helpless face, and Bastian's smile suddenly twisted into a hellish grin of mockery and confidently cruel domination. She felt lost and alone, the world of darkness reborn around her, silent eyes springing up around the bed, stoically observing the scene.

"Get off me!" She suddenly screamed, pushing hard into Bastian's naked chest. Everything was fucking naked, stripped for the laughing blackness to swallow up. "Get off!" She struck at him with all the strength she could muster, her fist rebounding from his taut ribcage. He staggered backwards, a confused expression on his face that Odette couldn't see.

"What's wrong?" He stammered, as Odette frantically tried to wrap her clothing back around her. The bed felt hot, scorchingly unbearable, as if hell's furnace had just been lit beneath it. Her face burned, and it didn't seem like her imagination.

"Odette, what's wrong?" Bastian took a tentative step forward, touching a hand to her shoulder.

"Get the fuck off me!" Odette screamed, batting the hand away frantically. Hot tears poured down her face, as she hastily pulled her shirt on, inside out. "Get the fuck away!" She stormed out the door, tripping twice on the stairs but somehow making it to the bottom, despite the blinding deluge of tears.

"Do you want me to take you home?" Bastian whispered quietly from the top of the stairs, his voice drowned out by Odette's inner clamour. She rushed out onto the street, trying to drink in the cold air as if it were medicine. The darkness was still there, but it had backed away a little, watching with muted snarls from afar. Her head pounded, her heart pounded, and for a moment she wondered if her veins would burst. And then she wished they would.

CHAPTER 27

selbstmordkunst

"Believe me now?" Anna wasn't exactly being comforting, but she was the best Odette could do in the aftermath of the disastrous events the night before. She could have talked to Marie, but her inherent distrust had prevented her.

"Men are all like that, sheepfuckers, grubbing little swine. They'll lie into your ear a thousand times just to get one fuck in. They think with their fucking dicks, and nothing else. Men's bodies are like, controlled by their dicks, and they just kind of mindlessly follow the dick around while it looks for something to fuck. And then it tells their mouth to spew a bunch of lies so that they get some fucking. Men don't really have souls."

"Fuck," Odette groaned, rubbing her forehead with both hands. Anna had been saying I-told-you-so for about two hours, and didn't seem to be growing weary of it yet.

"Here, I want you to have something," she said, abruptly cutting off her own tirade. "Call it a consolation gift."

"What is it?" Odette asked, instantly suspicious. Anna wasn't the greatest gift-giver in the world.

"Promise you won't freak," Anna demanded darkly.

"Why would I freak?"

"Just promise."

"Fine. I promise. Now what the fuck is it?"

Anna pulled a black handgun out of her purse, and presented the handle of it to Odette.

"What the fuck is that?" Odette screamed, almost jumping backwards.

"It's a Glock," Anna replied coolly. "And you promised you wouldn't freak. God, when are you going to learn to expect these things?"

"Why are you giving me a fucking gun?" Odette couldn't seem to bring her voice below the pitch of a scream, and she absolutely refused to sit back down. Fuck promises.

"Uh, to shoot someone. What do you think they invented guns for?"

"I can't take that, Anna," Odette's tone had grown a little less shrill, but no less panicky. "I can't. Where the fuck did you get that thing?"

"Why not?" Anna's face looked blank. "Here, I'll show you how to use it and everything."

"Do you know how much trouble I'll be in if Marie finds that in my room?"

"She goes in your room?"

"Well, no . . . not really . . . not that I know of, anyway," Odette took a trembling seat next to Anna, averting her eyes from the deadly little glistening killing toy in her hand.

"Then what the fuck are you worried about?"

"It's possible, OK?"

"Worry about the possibilities after you're fucking dead and there's nothing better to do."

"I can't take a fucking gun, Anna. It's fucking illegal. Where the fuck did you even get that thing?" Odette's voice was beginning to grow more shrill again, but she seemed to have lost the ability to control it.

"I know people," Anna smiled cruelly. "I don't recall you freaking this bad when me and Til shot you up with heroin, and that's illegal too."

"Well you two didn't exactly give me a fucking choice, now did you?"

"Just stop whining and take the fucking gun, please," Anna proffered the handle to Odette again. Odette accepted it gingerly, holding the hardwood grip with her finger-tips, watching it swing back and forth below her.

"You're not gonna be able to shoot it like that," Anna observed.

"I'm not going to shoot it," Odette scowled.

"Yes you are," Anna contradicted confidently.

"Just take it away, please, Anna," Odette pleaded.

"Just put it in your fucking bag, please, Odette."

"For Christ's sake, Anna," Odette argued shrilly, but she already knew she had lost. She hastily swept the gun into her little red sack, a glowering expression of resentment consuming her features.

"Don't forget to pull the trigger."

"Phone for you, Odette," Marie called from the bottom of the stairs.

"Who is it?" Odette answered. She stood and stared at the Glock, lying cold and evil on her bedspread. She wasn't about to keep it in her bag all the time, but she wasn't sure where to hide it. Sighing in frustration, she pushed it underneath her pillow and patted it down, before hurrying down the steps.

"Hello?" She asked, picking up the telephone from the table.

"Hey, Odette," Bastian's nervous voice came rattling through the wires.

"I don't wanna talk to you, Bastian."

"Please listen to me," his voice had a desperate tone in it that halted Odette from immediately hanging up. "I'm not trying to use you, or just get in your knickers, or anything like that. I really like you, I wish I hadn't have done it now. Please."

"Sorry," Odette whispered, lacking the steel she attempted to inject. "I can't trust you. I'm sorry."

CHAPTER 28

schlucken

The GMK was a place of trembling chaos, the leaderless Metropolitans failing in their desperate attempts to retain some semblance of order and organisation. Feelings of despair had soaked into all their hearts . . . what could they do without Alexander? Their prophet, their priest, their shining light, snuffed out in one moment of horrifying death. The masses still lay huddled, unattended, in the sea of hospital beds, coughing up trickles of plague-thickened oil. Odette stood in Alexander's place, before the door to the Tapestry Chamber, looking out over the scene of intense hopelessness. Nobody even seemed to notice her standing there, what few Metropolitans remained on their feet were entirely taken up with their meaningless attempts to comfort the dying. Odette felt the same sense of helplessness that she had felt when Alexander had first shown her the hospital. God or not, was there anything she could do here? She didn't even know why she was here,

221

perhaps it was just to watch the extinction of a species. A landmark event, surely.

Perhaps that was all her godlike status granted her, the ability to observe everything, impartial and uncaring, as the mortal ants died and battled and bled out their lives under her solemn gaze. She looked down at a white-coated doctor scurrying busily amongst the vast sea of patients that he could never hope to save. He was probably simply awaiting his turn, filling his mind with work to fight off any excessive foreboding. An end came for everyone, didn't it? No point in fretting about it, no matter how soon and inevitable the end was. Why would I even create these creatures? They were nothing like her, nothing . . . where was the proverbial image of God?

They were more like something from her nightmares, creatures of the darkness humanised with names and faces. And she felt compassion for them, pain even, watching them cough up their life force and die one by one. It was heart-rending for her. Diabolical or not, they were still her creations, her craft, her children. She stretched a hand out feebly over the sterilised white railing. Her slender fingers trembled over the vast expanse of death, darkened by the intense pale surrounding her. She wondered if she was as helpless here as she had been during the murder of Alexander, and if she had been brought here just to witness the product of her sick imagination. Her children cried out for her aid, pitiful little moans from broken retching chests, but still she heard each one clearly, ringing like a church bell in her tortured mind. How did she have the right to put creatures through this? To create a sentient race to serve as her divine playthings . . . how twisted must she be. Laughing as she dragged them to their respective dooms, stripping away all the pleasures she had granted in one ecstatic moment of agony and pain. She trivialised their lives into a game for her depraved amusement, she could see it all clearly now. Her eyelids flickered shut as she tried to feel the pain she had so callously inflicted on all of them, drink it up into her body so that it was hers and hers alone.

She gasped as the first spike struck her, searing through her body, ripping her nerves into clusters of raw persecution. Could this just be her imagination? She winced as a fresh wave of pain crashed through her frail body, churning her blood and tormenting her flesh. So cruel an imagination . . . Odette fell to the floor of the white walkway, her arms wrapped helplessly around her body as she contorted and convulsed to a thousand armies of agony, mercilessly hacking their crimson path through her nerves. Far below her she could hear a faint buzzing sound, the clamour of many surprised voices, revived with new hope.

Blood trickled out of Odette's mouth, tainting the colour-drained perfection surrounding her. The buzzing of flies, feeding off sickness and death, drowned out the other sounds in her ears as a black cloud descended upon her body. She could hear them sucking up her blood as it spattered on the floor, waiting for her to die. The pain never stopped, wave after wave of torment slashing apart her soul, devouring the frayed remnants of her sanity. Plague-thickened blood poured from her nose, coughed up from her stomach, blinding her pupils. It was almost black, congealed with death and tainted by disease.

The excited buzzing of the carrion-feeding flies grew and grew as she drew closer and closer to Death's gate. She could smell sulphur and hear the crackling of the hellish furnace, ashes covering her blindly darting eyes. The pain was threatening to consume her whole now, it had evolved into some monstrous creature with dripping jaws, rending her flesh and devouring it with blade-like teeth. Its foul breath blasted in her face as it crouched over her, acid dripping from its fangs onto her skin, burning little dark holes in the pale surface. How very Christlike.

The pain took a long time to fade away, and even when it had fully departed Odette could still feel the breath of the demonic creature caressing her skin. She was gone from the hospital, but she had seen the Metropolitans dancing and singing in gratitude for their national miracle. Every one of them healed, every trace of the Dark Blight banished from their bodies. Now she stood before the long table of Trifektum commanders, poignantly aware of the suspicion lurking in every pair of eyes.

"I don't think you should attack the GMK," she began timidly, and the suspicious looks intensified, some transforming into glares of open anger.

"Why not?" Lyneth demanded before she could speak again. The darkfeeder's tattoos glowed red in the candlelight.

"What is to be gained from a war? More Trifektum will die, and you won't be accomplishing anything," Odette was almost pleading, certain that they wouldn't listen to her advice.

"We didn't begin this war," Mordekai snapped. "Alexander did, when he burned our temples and stole our sacred artefacts. We only seek to reclaim what is ours, and every Trifektum soldier is willing to lay down their lives to see the Tapestry back in the hands of its rightful owners. Besides," he smirked, his long fingers pressed against the table. "This won't be a war . . . it will be a massacre."

"No, it will be a war," Odette tried to stand straighter, as if expecting a wind to blow her down. "The Metropolitans have discovered a cure for the Dark Blight. There will be a great deal of bloodshed if you attack the hospital."

The council table exploded into a raucous frenzy of commotion and shouting. Only Amelia, shrouded in her dark corner, remained calm.

"How do you know this?" Nayenna hissed after most of the noise had died down. Her many eyes rolled back and forth in her pasty white head, keeping every body in the room in her sight.

"I saw it," Odette replied coolly. Perhaps if they would not listen to her reason, they would listen to their own fear. "Every sick Metropolitan is cured. They have an army now."

The room erupted again. "Nonsense!" Several voices shouted, but there was a panicky edge to the word. Several of the commanders looked significantly less confident about their pending invasion, and there was talk of "options".

"Silence," Lyneth rasped, the glowing tattoos shifting and reforming under his skin. "Their numbers have already been greatly diminished by the plague. The hand of Our Lady is steering us towards inevitable victory. Even the Sapphire Werewolf has agreed to leave his eternal post to aid in finishing the Metropolitan problem once and for all. Cure or no cure, they will be helpless to stop us."

"But many of you will die," Odette protested, and she was starting to wonder if they even cared.

"If Our Lady requires our death in her service, who are we to deny her?" Lyneth replied calmly. "You have done a great deal to help us, child, and you have our gratitude, but you are no Trifektum commander. Whatever you are . . . sorceress, witch, demigoddess . . . you can not require that we ignore the commands of Our Lady."

"She doesn't want you to kill and she doesn't want you to die," Odette said desperately, casting swift glances around the table. The eyes staring back at her were hard, determined.

"Lyneth is right, child," Michael spoke slowly, as if unwilling to side with the Trifektum against his saviour. "The Metropolitans will never stop destroying our people, desecrating our religion, oppressing us into the earth. They are a plague upon us, as surely as the Dark Blight was a plague upon them. We must strike now, while they are still weak and in recovery. Cured or not, they will be unprepared for the battle that we will bring to their doorstep."

Odette closed her eyes, a long exhausted sigh escaping from between her lips. Why wouldn't they listen to her? Why did they insist on rushing to the death of thousands in such a pig-headed way?

When she opened her eyes, she was standing in a huge dark room. The commanders, the table, the flickering candles, were all gone. She could barely make out the vaulted ceiling high above and no walls were visible. The floor was made of stone, and it was so quiet that the ruffling of her clothing sounded loud. The vilest of scents assaulted her nostrils, overwhelming her so much with its ghastly odour that she almost vomited. Pinching her nostrils shut, she looked around, peering curiously into the darkness. There were pillars of carved stone surrounding her. Gargoyles and demons leered at her out of the darkness, cold grey eyes watching her every motion. She wasn't sure what to do, she took a timid step one way, then would stop and go another direction only to stop again and turn around in a circle. Then she began to hear a sound, incredibly soft at first, but slowly growing louder and louder until she could make out that it was two sounds, screaming, and a sad wailing song sung by many voices. Then it got close enough for her to hear the words of it.

Travelling forever down such a lonely road,
Surrounded by legions but always alone,
Bearing upon our backs such a heavy load,
Remember our candles that flickered and shone,
Snuffed out by time just as we,
Now to be bound by an iron chain,
Never again let us wander free,
Please hear our screams in the pouring rain,
The darkness will hide us if we can only fly,
Sheltering arms that await our return,
Hopelessly we weep and cry . . .

Suddenly the room Odette stood in was illuminated by a bright blue light that drifted around the pillars like a stream of banners in the air. Shimmering white figures, in the shape of skulls and disfigured heads, began to float upwards through the stones of the floor, into the blue light, which seemed to grow and grow as more spirits floated into it. Every head that floated past Odette turned in the air to look at her, their eyes replaced by abyssal black voids. She could hear the rattling sound of iron chains dragging across stone as the ghosts continued to sing their plaintive dirge. The rattling grew louder, like the singing, and then a ghostly skull appeared with a hook driven through its jaw. A long rusted chain, dripping blood, dangled behind it as it floated into the blue light. The screaming grew louder, until it was almost impossible to hear the words of the song over it. Odette covered her ears, but it did nothing to drown out the horrible noises. The blue light covered the whole ceiling now, brightly illuminating the vast room she stood in. There were huge stained glass windows high on the walls, looking out into pitch blackness. Each one of them was illustrated with portraits of death and despair, chained skeletons, bleeding heads mounted on spears, a ghastly figure with rotted flesh in a white robe, a pile of corpses being burned. She tore her eyes away from the windows, but the carvings and sculptures on the pillars were no less gory.

Then she noticed that the walls themselves were smeared with blood, and golden basins filled with blood and human organs stood at the base of each pillar. Skeletons and rotted corpses dangled by their necks on chains hanging from the roof, and there were bones scattered across the floor, shoved into big piles in the corner. Strips of human skin and chunks of bleeding flesh hung from hooks on the pillars. Odette collapsed to the floor, a cold sweat breaking out on her skin, and a loud pounding noise in her ears. Her stomach began to churn, and she tried to hold down her bile, but she couldn't. She closed her eyes as she lay on the ground, but she could still smell the foul stench, taste the vomit, and hear the screaming of the dead.

"What is this place?" she whispered, still keeping her eyes tight shut, as little respite as that was.

"It's the Cathedral of Death," a sepulchral voice echoed behind her, followed by the sound of wood tapping against stone. Odette whirled around to face a ghastly figure; a skull with faded brown skin stretched tight over its surface, blue lights blazing in its eye cavities. It wore a hooded red robe and clutched a gnarled deadwood staff in the bony fingers of its left hand. It threw its head back to reveal long black hair flowing down from the top of the skull.

"Who are you?" Odette gasped, bones rattling around her as she scrambling backwards.

"Tisk, tisk, so many questions," the foul apparition croaked, limping forward a couple steps, leaning heavily on its staff. Then it stopped, and grinned broadly, a horrible sight. "I'm Death, obviously."

"Am I dead?" Odette asked, trying to catch her breath.

"Again with the questions," Death groaned. "I swear I'm going to be replaced by a receptionist someday. And no, you can't die . . . not here, anyway. You are more fragile elsewhere. But here . . . I'm the only thing you see right now that you did not create. I have added a few touches though, I'll admit."

Odette scrabbled to her feet, dusting herself off. She did her best not to look around, the images of gore just sickened her. Several more questions sprang to her lips, but she visibly swallowed them down.

"Ask away, little goddess," Death grimaced, leaning on his staff.

"Why am I here?" Odette demanded, starting to feel a little more secure. Comfortable would be too much to ask in a hellish place like this.

"That I can not answer," the apparition answered. "But I will suggest that it would be amiss for you not to view this visit with a certain sense of . . . foreboding. But I am a simple shepherd, not a prophet."

"You mean I could die?"

Death shrugged, taking a seat on a stone bench that sat beneath one of the pillars. A basin of blood, collecting red drips that fell from the roof, stood beside it. "People die all the time," he said. "Gods . . . not quite so often."

"You said I didn't create you," Odette said, walking forward. "If I didn't, who did? And why are you here, in my world?"

"Death is everywhere," the robed figure answered, looking off into the darkness. His voice took on a vaguely wistful tone. "I am in every child's dreams, whether they remember it or not. I am invested in every little deed, every twist, every motion, of humanity, and thus I am present in every creation of that species. And, child, you are human, and no matter how long you flee from that fact, one day it will overtake you with jarring force."

"I'm not running away," Odette said defensively. "I never asked for this. I don't remember creating anything, I just fell in the middle of it."

"You don't remember . . ." Death looked at her with a strange smile on his face. "Well it was a long time ago. We are all flawed in some way. Even I am just a product of humanity's collective imagination, the manifestation of their fear of their own demise. Hence my soul-harrowing appearance. Human thought can be shockingly powerful."

"Do you mean that all of this . . . the Trifektum, the Metropolitans . . . it's all real?"

"When you are as old as me, and someday, child, you will be, you will stop worrying about what is real and what is not," Death spoke slowly, tapping his staff three times on the stones. "Reality is something humans cling to, a crutch if you will. They are afraid to venture beyond the vision of their comfortable horizons. So your race has always been, and so they always will be, but you will also always have your pioneers, those fascinated by the darkness and the unknown. And they have always dragged the unwilling masses through the screens of their happy realities. Look at all their fears and misconceptions of death. How do they live their whole lives with that sort of foreboding hanging over their head? Comfort and denial are perhaps what humans are attracted to the most."

"What is death like?" Odette asked, sitting down on the bench next to the manifestation. She felt her fear of this place slowly evaporating.

"Ah, I never said there should be no mysteries," Death smiled down at her. "Without mysteries, there can be no hunger. But there is no need to fear the mysterious, no need to shrink away from it. Look at how most humans can not even begin to understand those of their kind who commit suicide. But perhaps those who take their own lives can be said to be merely . . . curious." Death laid his skeletal fingers on Odette's shoulder. "I would love to stay and chat but people are dying like flies and you know how most people have to be led by the nose." He laughed, a harsh, echoing sound. Then he grew serious, moving his hand to the top of Odette's head. "Remember child, that no matter what happens, no one can take your immortality."

CHAPTER 29

am horizont

Odette had prayed that Bastian wouldn't talk to her at school today, but God, as usual, seemed disinterested in granting any of her requests.

"Hey, Odette," he wasn't wearing his usual array of smiles. bastard.

"Go away, Bastian," Odette answered without looking up.

"I'm really sorry about what happened," he was almost stammering. Was he scared or something? What the fuck did he have to be scared of? "I . . . I thought you wanted to, I'm really sorry."

"What I want is to never see you again," Odette snarled, pushing past him into the crowded. "Leave me alone." How could he have done that to her? She had trusted him so much. Fucking pigs.

Odette and Anna sat silently together after school, passing a cigarette back and forth. Anna seemed very disinterested in talking, all she did was sit and look at up at the sky, as if she was searching for something.

"Do you think God is real?" she finally asked, without looking down.

"No," Odette replied quickly, with more certainty in her mind than she felt in her voice. "If he is real, then he's a twisted evil bastard."

"Agreed," Anna passed the cigarette back to Odette. She looked almost unreal, like something from a hallucination or a dream. She turned and looked at Odette, and stars sparkled in her eyes. "What did you do with that gun I gave you?"

"I . . ." Odette was caught off guard. "I put it under my pillow, like you told me to."

"Oh, good," Anna sounded genuinely relieved. "I was afraid you might have thrown it away or something."

"If Marie finds it I'm going to be in so much trouble . . ."

"Don't worry about that," Anna cut her off, a ghost of a smile playing on her face. "When she finds it you won't have to worry about stupid shit like that anymore."

Odette wanted to ask her what she meant, but decided it was better to bite back the question. She wasn't sure she wanted to know.

"That Dieter guy . . ." Anna began slowly. Odette felt her spine stiffen, as Anna's eyes turned on her again, surveying her almost lazily. "You would tell me if there was any really bad shit going on, right? I mean . . . you can tell me anything, you know."

Odette started to shake her head, tears springing to the back of her eyes. She was so sick of lying. "Odette, stop the fucking bullshit," Anna suddenly screamed, grabbing ahold of her shoulders. "I know what he did to you, OK? I already know."

"How?" Odette's voice trembled and distorted the word. Tears were flowing now, and she made no effort to stop them.

"Because he raped me, Odette, OK? Why do you think I gave you the goddamn gun?"

Odette's head dropped, she couldn't stare into Anna's burning eyes any longer. There was a madness there that she couldn't face.

"Listen to me, Odette, listen. We have to kill him."

Her head snapped up. Her lips inaudibly formed the word what, suddenly helpless to produce sound.

"Listen. He's a monster, he has to be put down OK? Just like a fucking dog. Just like that. We have to kill Dieter. How many times has he done it to you, Odette? Ten . . . twenty . . . a hundred? He isn't going to stop, not ever. He'll keep doing it over and over until you can't even look at yourself in the mirror without puking."

"Can't we tell someone?" Odette whispered.

"Who the fuck are we going to tell, Odette? Cops? Teachers? I don't trust any of those pigfuckers, and I know you don't either. Why would they believe us? We're crazy, we're problems, we're little menaces running around ruining their perfect little streamlined world. We are going to take that gun and we are going to shoot Dieter through the head with it."

"We'll get caught. Anna, we'll get caught. OK, we'll get caught, and then what?"

Anna smiled. "You can't catch the dead. I want a front-row seat to watch him burn in hell."

"Anna . . . no . . . I can't . . ."

"Yes you can," Anna snapped ferociously. "Come on, you and me, going down together. And then we get to watch him burn. Live together, die together."

Odette shook her head frantically, blinded by a new deluge of tears. She felt exhausted, she couldn't argue anymore.

"You have the gun," Anna whispered cajolingly. "Don't let him hurt you anymore. Don't let him."

"OK," Odette felt detached from her own body, watching her lips mindlessly repeating what Anna wanted her to hear. "Fine. I'll do it." What do I have to live for anyway?

"What are you doing?" Amelia was crouched beside her, an unreadable expression in her hard blue eyes. Odette stared into them for a long moment, falling into the frigid pools. Dying of hypothermia. Then she simply shook her head and looked away.

"Are you trying to destroy the world?" Amelia persisted, grabbing ahold of Odette's arm. Odette looked around desperately, but she couldn't see Anna anymore. White fog swirled everywhere, obscuring her vision.

"I really don't think the world is going to be destroyed by the death of one sad little mad girl," she snapped cynically.

"Not yours," Amelia answered. "Ours."

"Your world isn't real, it never has been. You aren't even real. I'm insane."

"And yet I'm standing right in front of you."

"Because I'm insane," Odette reiterated.

"Michael has declared you to be a fraud and charlatan, and a Metropolitan spy," Amelia continued, ignoring her assertions. "We're moving on the GMK within the next twenty-four hours. To destroy it, once and for all."

"Why should I care?"

"I just thought you might."

"Well, I don't," Odette turned away, wrapping her arms around her body. "Why should it matter to me if thousands of imaginary people start slaughtering each other? The only real blood being shed is mine."

When she turned back, Amelia had disappeared and Anna was sitting there, staring at her quizzically.

"I'll do it," Odette repeated.

CHAPTER 30

die tore des paradieses

Odette drifted in the cold air at the outskirts of the Yellow Forest, one with the piercing wind and the curling mist. She didn't feel the elements, she had no skin with which to do so, but she could tell somehow by looking at it. She only wondered for a moment what she was doing here before the bushes started crashing with the movements of a vast number of creatures, an army. Amelia herself was the first to emerge from the line of trees, the Key sheathed across her back and a pine-wood torch in her left hand. Her murderous blue eyes had that same hard determined look they had worn before the assassination of Alexander.

Members of the council and their body guards came striding behind her, Michael, Nicholas with Krysis hanging out across his lips, flat evil eyes staring straight ahead and forked tongue pulsating, Lyneth, tattoos hidden by a full set of spiked black battle armour, Mordekai, Nayenna, her many multi-faceted eyes rolling back and forth in glee. Behind them came the full force of the Trifektum, humans, darkfeeders, otherkin, the spider clan, all armoured and bristling with weaponry, the light of war burning in their eyes. Two huge drums rolled out their booming melody from the centre of the column, slowly beating out the steps to the dance of death. Smoke curled back over the battle-ready horde, dancing gracefully around the banners that flapped raggedly in the rush of the wind. In the distance Odette could see the Hospital, the concrete walls and barbed wire of the compound that surrounded it filled with the legions of healed Metropolitans. A fanatic light burned in their eyes, the fanaticism of those sure that God is on their side. Why else would she have healed them after all, if not to rid the world of the menace of blood?

"Odette?"

"Odette?"

Odette looked up into the eyes of a teacher whose name she had forgotten. She couldn't ever remember the names of boring people.

"Do you want to come with me, Odette?" the teacher asked. "The police want to talk to you." Super.

The two policemen looked big, and menacing, and disturbingly real.

"Odette Braun?" the thinner of them asked, in a grave tone.

"Yeah."

"Do you know an Anna Schweiger?" A wave of fear shot through Odette.

"Yes," she answered slowly, trying to keep the rising panic out of her voice. She wasn't sure if she succeeded. "Did something happen to her?"

The policeman coughed uncertainly. This couldn't be normal protocol. "Her body was found in the river about four hours ago. A suicide note was found pinned to the mirror in her room. It's addressed to you."

Odette felt colourless, courses of shock running through her veins. She hadn't believed Anna would actually do it. "What . . . what does it say?" she stammered. The policeman stoically handed a scrawled note to her. It almost slipped through her shaking fingers when she tried to grab it.

Dear Odette,

b.s.i. I wanted to do it for you, but I couldn't. I'm sorry. I'm actually wondering now about all the bullshit my parents spewed about "happier places". I guess I'll find out soon enough. I'm really sorry.

Love,
Anna (b.s.i.)

P.S. Use what I gave you.

Odette pushed open the front door of the Schiller's house and stumbled upstairs. She saw Dieter sitting in his recliner out of the corner of her eye and knew he would be following her upstairs soon. She slammed her bedroom door behind her, battling to see through the rush of tears that kept blinding her. She grabbed her pillow and threw it down on the ground, revealing the deadly Glock, the hard black gun contrasted sharply with the soft white sheets it lay on. She gritted her teeth decisively and swept up the gun into her right hand, turning around to face the door. She heard the steps creaking as Dieter came walking up them slowly, and a new wave of tears came streaming out of her eyes. She wiped them away, trying to fight them back; she had to be able to see, for Anna. She raised the gun up, holding the brown grip in both hands. The world swam around her, a chaotic buzzing assailed her ears, like a thousand bees swarming around her head. She swallowed and her own spit tasted bitter, tainted. She braced herself, pushing away all the things distracting her, incapacitating her. Her door handle slowly turned. She raised the Glock so that the barrel pointed where she knew Dieter's head would be.

The door swung open, with agonising torpor. She could see a glimpse Dieter through the hinges; he was wearing a brown shirt, she hadn't noticed that downstairs. She could hear his footfalls echoing through her mind as he took one step forward, then another, but still barricaded by the door. Then he emerged into her line of vision, one hand on the door to shut it behind him so that Odette would be trapped inside with him. Odette didn't speak, she just closed her eyes and squeezed the trigger. The gun blast shocked her, it reverberated throughout her mind, drowning out and wiping away her chaotic thoughts. Through the waves of its deafening sound, she heard another; the sound of a heavy body hitting the floor. She slowly fluttered her eyelids open; Dieter's body was dead and already cooling, a large red splattered circle on the wall the only remnant of his life.

The Glock sat on the bed next to Odette, its black barrel gleaming softly in the half-light. Odette didn't look at it, or at the warm corpse crumpled in her doorway, she stared straight ahead, tears staining her pale cheeks.

"What are you doing?" Amelia stood crouched on the floor, a look of terror shooting across her features. "Odette . . . I can feel it. This horrible shock will destroy our world."

Odette turned her weeping eyes to the Archmurderer. "It's not real," she whispered. "None of it can be."

"You're real," Amelia answered, her gaze taking in the loaded pistol on the bed. "You are our goddess. How will we survive without you? What will happen to all of us? Don't abandon us all because some fools abandoned you."

"Anna was real," Odette's breath caught in her throat. She could still barely stand to say the name. Amelia took a step forward, stretching out her hand. Odette closed her eyes, only for a moment. Tears still squeezed out of her eyelids, running down her face. When she snapped them open, Amelia was gone, leaving only the cold empty room. Odette's hand reached out for the handle of the gun, her fingers wrapping around the hardwood grips. She raised it trembling until the barrel was pressed against her short black hair. She could hear voices screaming in the back of her head, Alexander's hoarse yelling, Rabbit, and the soft sound of Amelia crying, her hard exterior finally broken. Then, drowning out all the rest, she heard Death's soft reassuring whispers. I guess Nietzsche was right, God is dead. She killed herself.